THE Exceptional MAGGIE CHOWDER

RENEE BEAUREGARD LUTE

ILLUSTRATED BY LUNA VALENTINE

ALBERT WHITMAN & COMPANY
CHICAGO, ILLINOIS

Library of Congress Cataloging-in-Publication
data is on file with the publisher.
Text copyright © 2020 by Renee Beauregard Lute
Illustrations copyright © 2020 by Albert Whitman & Company
Illustrations by Luna Valentine
First published in the United States of America
in 2020 by Albert Whitman & Company
ISBN 978-0-8075-3678-0 (hardcover)
ISBN 978-0-8075-3679-7 (ebook)

Printed in the United States of America
10 9 8 7 6 5 4 3 2 1 LB 24 23 22 21 20

Design by Valerie Hernández

For more information about Albert Whitman & Company,
visit our website at www.albertwhitman.com.

To Zach Lute, who is one heck of a husband, dad, editor, support system, and chili chef. And to Maddie, Simon, and Cecily, who inspire me all the time.—RBL

To my mum, Joanna, and my agent, Alex; two amazing women who inspire me every day to be strong and believe in myself, no matter what life throws at me. Thank you for being my superheroines!—LV

THE WORLD OF
THE EXCEPTIONAL EAGIRL

EAGIRL

RANGER DANGER

POSSUM SAUCE

GRIZZLY BAIRD

BOSSTRICH

OSPREY GIRL

BAIRD CUBS

FOREST FIERA

"Good things are going to happen this summer," I say. "Great things. Exceptional things." It's the first day of summer break, and I can just tell.

"You're usually not this upbeat at the beginning of summer," Mom says.

She's right. My best friend, LaTanya, is going away to Vancouver with her family for the whole beginning of the summer, just like she does every summer. Her dad is the assistant coach for a football team there. Mom is going to drive me to LaTanya's house for the afternoon so we can make friendship bracelets, which *some* people think is doofy, but LaTanya and I don't care what other people think. When you're twelve and you don't have your own phone, which I don't, Vancouver is basically as far away from Renton as Australia, but LaTanya and I are solid. And I refuse to let Vancouver or football ruin my summer.

"I'm experimenting with optimism," I say. "Like Eagirl in *The Exceptional Eagirl #62* when she tries to be more like Possum Sauce."

"Possum Sauce is the sidekick?" asks Mom. "I can never keep them straight. In any case, I'm all for optimism this summer."

Mom goes back downstairs, leaving me to finish packing. I stuff my case of bracelet floss and beads into an Eagirl tote bag I got at the comic book store downtown last winter. When I bought it, the bald guy behind the counter snorted and said, "Eagirl? Isn't she some kinda forest ranger superhero?"

"Yeah," I said. "She is." I put my money on the counter and glared at him like Eagirl would.

He handed me my tote bag and didn't say anything after that. Probably because of my intimidating Eagirl glare. Or maybe because he remembered he was wearing a Shrimpman T-shirt, and Shrimpman is the *worst* superhero. He's not even a superhero. He's Lobsterman's sidekick. I try not to yuck other people's yums, but Shrimpman really is the worst. He's an actual shrimp man.

I'm going to be just like Eagirl one day, except I wasn't raised by eagles. I'm going to become a forest ranger. I'll uphold the law of the forest and assist those who need help, like she does.

"Maggie!" Mom calls from downstairs. "Almost ready to go?"

"Just a sec!" I yell back.

I pack a small brown teddy bear wearing a Seattle shirt into my tote, too. I bought it for LaTanya at the drugstore. They didn't have any teddy bears wearing Renton shirts, and Seattle is the next closest city. I'm giving it to LaTanya in case she gets homesick when she's in Vancouver, which she always does.

It's raining lightly outside my bedroom windows, and everything in the yard looks fresh and green. Our yard backs up to the woods, so if I look out my window long enough, I almost always see a small, black squirrel racing up a tree or a silvery-blue Steller's jay belching *behhh, behhh, behhh* from a conifer branch. When I'm lucky, I can spot a deer, or even a whole family of deer. Once there was a little black bear pawing at one of our suet feeders. Mom didn't think he was as awesome as I did.

I swing my tote bag onto my shoulder and head down the stairs to the kitchen. Mom is in there, wearing her HOT CHOWDAH apron and crouching to look at something baking in the oven. Dad bought back Mom that apron when he was in Boston on a business trip. It's kind of funny because our last name is Chowder. He brought back taffy for me and my four-year-old brother, Aaron. Dad travels a lot on business, but he's been home with us this whole week, which is nice.

His job sounds boring—he's a business-development-something-something at a software company—but he's never boring when he talks about it. He does an impression of his boss that makes me and Aaron laugh until we nearly pee our pants. Dad pulls his pants up really high and rubs the top of his head and says, "Oh ah, well ah, these numbahs aren't what we're lookin' for, bustah. Not what we're lookin' for at all. Can we get some bettah numbahs?"

"What are you making?" I ask Mom.

"Corn bread." The oven beeps, and Mom turns it off. She pulls a round pan out and sets it on top of the stove. "To have with our chili tonight. Are you eating dinner with LaTanya's family?"

"Yeah."

"Okay." She brushes her hands on the apron and tosses it onto the counter. "I'm ready to go when you are!" She cups her hands around her mouth and yells into the living room. "Aaaaron, time to get in the caaaaar!"

Aaron trots into the kitchen with his eyes on a piece of paper.

"What do you have?" Mom asks.

"My list," says Aaron, still looking at the paper. I look over his shoulder. His list is actually a grocery-store receipt.

"Bananas," I read out loud. "Cottage cheese, grapes, pretzels, ground beef."

Aaron smiles at me appreciatively. "Frozen corn, deli ham, butter."

"You're a good reader, Aaron," I say. Aaron is the only kid in his preschool class who can read. He is also the only kid in his preschool class who gets sent home with "couldn't sit still during circle time" notes almost every day.

Aaron is four years old, and he's autistic. That means he has some *unusual and wonderful qualities*, which is how Dad puts it. Aaron is really awesome at spelling and reading, and he loves making lists as much as I love Eagirl. When he's excited or having trouble with something he's feeling (like wet socks), he stims. For Aaron, that means jumping up and down or wiggling his fingers in front of his eyes. Or both. I think it's super cute, but it can be a little alarming if you're not used to it. I'm *very* used to it.

Aaron scowls at me because I stopped reading from his list.

"Carrots," he says. "Hummus. Goldfish crackers."

"Milk and bagels," I say.

"Let's load up," says Mom.

Aaron carefully folds his receipt and tucks it into the pocket of his shorts.

On the short ride to LaTanya's house, he pulls it out again. "Bananas, cottage cheese, grapes, pretzels," he reads.

LaTanya's house is my favorite house, besides *my* house. Hers is a small red trilevel across from Petrovitsky Park. There are always good snacks, and we're allowed to eat them, even while LaTanya's mom is cooking dinner. My mom never lets us snack before dinner.

LaTanya flings her front door wide open. "Hot fudge sundaes and manicures? We've got a lot of stuff to do and not much time!"

I follow her into the warm kitchen. LaTanya's mom is rinsing a bowl in the sink.

"Mmm, it smells good in here," I say. "What is it?"

"Pot roast," says LaTanya's mom, "so don't fill up *too* much on your sundaes." She winks at us.

LaTanya's mom is my favorite mom, besides *my* mom. She never yells, and she is a very good cook. My mom says she looks like a movie star, but I think she looks like Dahlia, Queen Warrior from the *Dahlia, Queen Warrior* comics. Dahlia is LaTanya's favorite superhero. She even went to a casting call when they made the *Dahlia, Queen Warrior* movie. LaTanya wanted to play Dahlia's daughter, Princess Calluna. She didn't get the part, but she did get to meet the woman who plays Dahlia. She got her autograph on a gum wrapper, and it's her most prized possession.

LaTanya scoops vanilla ice cream into two cold bowls

she pulled out of the freezer. That's a trick her mom taught us—it's so the ice cream doesn't start melting right away. "I'm going to paint my nails black and orange for the Lions," she says. The BC Lions are the football team LaTanya's dad coaches in Vancouver.

I study my nails. They're short and uneven because I bite them. "I'll paint mine blue and green for the Seahawks." The Seattle Seahawks are a pretty big deal around here. During football season, all the store owners in Renton put out blue and green balloons. Aaron likes the mascot a lot. He would appreciate blue and green nails.

LaTanya's mom points a spatula at us. "You know, LaTanya, you might want to think about blue and green nails, too. For luck."

LaTanya sighs. "Daddy is still dreaming of coaching the Seahawks," she says to me.

"Without dreams, nobody has much," says her mom. "Remember that. And if Daddy has a dream, then we all do, because family members support each other." She squeezes LaTanya's shoulders. LaTanya's mom always says smart things like that. And she's usually right about everything.

LaTanya pulls a jar of homemade hot fudge out of the refrigerator and pops it into the microwave. "Blue and green nails it is," she says. Her mom smiles at her.

Once our nails are dry, we sit on the floor of LaTanya's

bedroom threading beads together. The bracelet I'm making for LaTanya says V-E-R-Y-B-E-S-T. When I feel around in my tote for the wire clasp that goes on the end of the bracelet, I feel the little brown bear.

"Oh! I forgot. I got this for you." I hand the bear to LaTanya.

LaTanya studies the bear, and then hugs it to her chest.

"Thanks, Maggie. You're my very best. That's why the bracelet I'm making says *very best.*"

"Whoa!" I show her the bracelet I'm making for her. "So does mine."

"Brain twins," says LaTanya.

"Girls!" LaTanya's mom calls from downstairs. "Time for dinner!"

✖✖✖

After dinner, Mom pulls up in front of LaTanya's house. Aaron is in the car, and he hates getting in and out of his booster seat a bunch of times, so Mom waits for me to come out.

LaTanya and I give each other the longest, tightest hug in the history of hugs.

"I'm gonna miss you," she says.

"I'm gonna miss you too." I jangle my new bracelet around on my wrist. "I'll wear it the whole time you're gone."

LaTanya holds up her wrist. "Same."

LaTanya's mom opens the door. "It's only a month, girls! We'll be back before you know it." She waves to my mom in the driveway and holds one finger up like *Maggie will be out in one minute*. "It's going to be a great summer. For all of us."

LaTanya's mom is usually right about everything. I hope she's right about this summer, too.

On normal Saturdays, I eat waffles for breakfast and read an Eagirl comic and go shopping with Mom. That's what I do this Saturday morning, too. I have waffles for breakfast. And I read *The Exceptional Eagirl #16*. That's the one where Eagirl's sidekick, Possum Sauce, wrestles a kidnapper and rescues a bus full of kids. And now I'm going shopping with Mom.

Aaron hates shopping. He only likes T-shirts from Target. He has all the exact same ones, in all different colors. That's because Target T-shirts don't have tags in them. Aaron hates tags *and* waiting in line, so Mom and I shop alone.

He's pretty much always been who he is, but we didn't know there was a name for it until he got a diagnosis last year. I think for a while my parents didn't really know what to do with that, so things just kind of stayed the same. But recently things have been a little harder for Aaron, and his doctor suggested some therapies he could start this summer.

I skip down the brick steps of our white house and through the rows of giant trees that shade our driveway, stopping to heroically move some worms off the wet sidewalk before it dries. We had a big storm last night, and worms are always all over the sidewalk after a storm.

The trees are still dripping on me as I climb into the passenger side of Mom's dark-green car and shut the door. Before I click my seat belt buckle, Mom makes a disapproving *mmm* sound from the driver's seat.

"Maggie, it's safer in the back seat. Can you please humor me?"

I lean my head back into the headrest. "But we're having a Mom and Maggie day. We're bonding. How are we supposed to bond if I'm sitting in the back and you're driving me around in the driver's seat? People in the back of police cars don't bond with their drivers. Kids going to prom don't bond with *their* drivers. People—"

Crack.

Crack.

Craaaaack.

It happens fast and slow at the same time. One of the big, old trees next to our driveway breaks in half. The top half *whooshes* down onto the car. I hear a thud. The sound of crumpling metal. And then I hear screaming.

The screaming sounds far away at first, but then closer. I look at Mom. The screaming is coming from her.

"Oh my God, oh my *God*," Mom shrieks. Her whole body is shaking. She fumbles with her seat belt, gives up, and leans over to cup my face in her hands. "My baby girl, oh my God, are you okay? Are you okay?"

I try to nod, but she is really squeezing my face hard. Big tears roll down her freckled cheeks. Strands of brown hair have escaped from her braid and stick to the sweat on her jaw and neck.

"I'm okay. I'm fine. Are you?"

She closes her eyes and nods, but she doesn't seem okay.

"We're fine, Mom." I unbuckle my seat belt and hug her tight. She squeezes me back, and I can feel her breath slowing down.

We pull apart and turn at the same time. The fallen tree has completely crushed the back seat. Tiny pieces of glass are all over the floor and the seat.

This is exactly the kind of thing that would happen to Eagirl. Well, not exactly. She would have stopped the tree from falling in the first place. Or she would have saved a kid's life from the—

Hold on. *I* saved a kid's life from the tree.

"Whoa, Mom," I say. "If I'd got into the back seat like you told me to, I would have—"

"No!" Mom yelps. Her face crumples up, and she presses it onto the steering wheel. Her back heaves as she cries.

"Hey, but I *didn't*," I say. I put a hand on her back. "And I'm fine! I just meant…"

Uh-oh. I made it worse. Eagirl never makes things worse. Only better.

Dad and Aaron appear in the windshield.

"Oh my God," yells Dad. We can hear him clearly because the back seat and rear windows have all been shattered. He is gesturing widely with his hands. At the car, then the tree, then back at the car again. "Are you two okay? What *happened?*"

Mom looks up from the steering wheel. "What do you *mean* 'what happened?' What does it look like?"

"We're fine," I add quickly.

"Oh my God," Dad says again. He presses his fingers into his forehead. "Thank God no one was in the back seat."

Mom collapses into the steering wheel again, sobbing.

Aaron walks over to my window. He sighs. "A broken car," he says, shaking his head sadly. "A broken tree."

My stomach cramps up as I look back at the crumpled remains of Aaron's booster seat, covered in glass…and tree. Aaron would have been killed if he had come with us. It is so lucky that Aaron hates shopping.

"Why," Mom asks the steering wheel. "Why *today?*

Why right now?" She looks up at Dad through the windshield. "I guess our decision has been made *for* us."

Dad nods slowly at Mom.

What decision? I look back and forth from Mom to Dad.

"A broken car," says Aaron, surveying the back seat. "This car is broken."

"This car *is* broken," I say. I look at Mom. "What decision?"

"We'll talk about it tonight, okay? At dinner. When we're all together. It's going to be okay. We'll talk about it tonight."

At the end of *The Exceptional Eagirl #22*, Eagirl is supposed to meet Possum Sauce and Grizzly Baird for Thanksgiving dinner. When she arrives at Possum's lair, it's empty, and she knows something terrible has happened. I feel a little like Eagirl in that last panel.

3

We're having buffalo-chicken pasta salad for dinner. Aaron is having his without the "buffalo" part or the celery part because he doesn't like spicy stuff or green vegetables. He gets carrot sticks on the side instead. I don't like celery either, but my bowl has celery in it because life is not fair to older siblings.

I usually like the parts of buffalo-chicken pasta salad that aren't the celery parts, but tonight my stomach feels sick. It's felt sick ever since the car. I hate seeing my mom cry, and I hate not knowing important things. What's going on? What are we going to talk about during dinner? Mom and Dad are just eating their food like nothing's wrong. If they don't start talking soon, I'm going to explode. I stab a chicken chunk with my fork, but I don't put it in my mouth.

"My milk," whimpers Aaron. He's been drinking out of his straw all wrong. There's a quarter-sized wet spot on the front of his shirt where his milk dripped. No matter how many times Mom and Dad and I tell him to hold his cup straight up and down, Aaron tips his cup toward him when he's drinking out of a straw. "My *milk*!" he squeals. His face crumples, and he sets his cup down hard on the table.

Here we go.

You know the saying, "Don't cry over spilled milk"? Well, Aaron's heard that saying about a million times, and he's still literally crying over it. Nobody yelled at him. He didn't even spill that much. But that doesn't make any difference to Aaron.

"My *milk*! My milk my milk my milk my—"

"Shh, buddy. You're just fine." Mom rubs the milk spot on Aaron's shirt with her napkin.

Aaron is breathing fast. He looks down at his shirt. "My milk," he says very quietly. "My milk my milk my milk my milk. I spilled my milk."

Mom sighs. She raises her eyebrows at Dad. Dad raises his eyebrows back at Mom.

"Well, it's been a loooong, wild day," I say. "Hasn't it? Oh! That reminds me. What were we all going to talk about at dinner?" I smile as nonchalantly as I can from Mom to Dad and back to Mom.

"I spilled my milk," says Aaron. He doesn't seem as upset anymore. He inspects his plate. He picks a noodle out of his pasta salad and pops it into his mouth. "My milk. I spilled my milk."

"Don't talk with your mouth full," I say. But I really mean *Don't talk at all*, because I'm trying to get Mom and Dad to spill the beans before they get distracted again.

Dad clears his throat. "We've got some news." He makes a tight-mouthed smile at Mom. That means it's probably bad news.

I take a deep breath. In *The Exceptional Eagirl #19*, Ranger Danger tells Eagirl that he has news. He's found her biological mother. But he makes the tight-mouth smile that my dad just did, because Eagirl's biological mother is her greatest enemy: Forest Fiera. That's the smile you do when you have bad news.

"It isn't exactly bad news," Mom says.

I let out a breath.

"We're just going to need you to be really flexible. We're all going to need to adjust to some changes." Mom glances at Aaron as she continues. "And we know Aaron sometimes has a hard time with changes, right, Aaron?"

"Right, Aaron!" he answers.

"We're all going to need to be patient and help him adjust, too, okay?"

Flexible? I can be flexible. I was practically born flexible. They can call me Flexigirl: The Girl Who Adjusts. I take another breath and channel Eagirl. Eagirl can handle anything, and so can I. Eagirl would help Aaron adjust.

"Try me," I say. I lay my fork down on my napkin. "What changes?"

Dad rubs his hands together like a magician. He gets really dramatic sometimes. He looks pleased with himself. "Last Thursday, I lost my job."

"You...lost your job?" I look from Dad to Mom. Dad looks almost happy about it. Mom is smiling kind of a tight smile.

"I sure did," Dad says. "But we decided to see it as an opportunity. You know that Aaron starts his therapies next week. And he starts developmental preschool in the fall. Back when we had two unsquashed cars and one income, your mom was going to take him to all of that while I worked at a job that I really didn't love. Now, things are different. I don't have that job anymore, and we don't have a second car anymore."

"You lost your job," I say again. "And we lost our car." No job and no green car.

"Right," says Dad. "And at first, I was really freaked out about it. But you know what? Now I can get Aaron where he needs to go and pursue a dream I've had since childhood." He stares dramatically at the ceiling above my head and spreads his hands out like he's at the end of a musical number.

"Your dream was to be a chauffeur?" I ask.

Dad snaps out of his weird ceiling-staring moment. "No! My dream was—is—to be an actor." He pronounces the word *actor* like it rhymes with *back door*.

"You're going to be an actor?" I say. "Like, in movies?"

I can imagine Dad being an actor. His impression of his boss—er, old boss, I guess—is very funny. And it would be cool to see Dad in movies. It would be extra cool if he brought me to red-carpet movie premieres, and I got to meet all kinds of celebrities and get my makeup done by a professional even before I turn thirteen, because everybody wears makeup at movie premieres.

Dad chuckles. "Maybe someday, Mags, but for now, I've got a callback for a web series."

A web series doesn't sound like something with a red-carpet premiere.

"It'll be on the internet. It's very low-budget, so I won't get paid much, but it'll be a great experience, if I get the part. It's for a modern retelling of *Lyle, Lyle, Crocodile*. You know, the kids' book about the family that inherits a crocodile with their house? It's going to be really wild."

My chest fills with that disappointed feeling I got when I thought I was having a surprise birthday party last year, but instead I got surprised with a birthday visit from

Grandma Barrel, who told me I was too old to read comic books. She bought me a suitcase with a couple of old, used books inside, and Mom said, "Is this a passive-aggressive way of asking us to send her to Arizona for a visit? Because I told you she is afraid to fly alone!" I'm not actually afraid to fly alone, but I don't want to visit Grandma Barrel by myself. She's the kind of grandmother who tells you you're too old for things and who gives you a suitcase for your birthday.

Dad grins at me. "You'll never guess what part I was called back for."

I bet I can guess.

Dad holds up one finger and runs out of the dining room. When he comes back, he is holding a very fake-looking green crocodile snout. It looks like something Aaron would make. The teeth stick out in all different directions.

"Lyle! I got called back for the part of Lyle!" Dad is beaming. He looks really excited. I don't feel even a little excited about this, but I smile anyway.

I still have a weird feeling. If Dad lost his job, and his new maybe-job doesn't pay very much, and Mom doesn't make any money because she stays home and takes care of us and the house, then how are we going to—

"So, there's another big change," says Mom. "Are you doing okay so far? You seem like you're doing okay."

"I'm doing okay," I say. Eagirl would be doing okay.

So I am doing okay. This is kind of like when Ranger Danger disappears, and Eagirl has to stay strong and take over his post until Possum Sauce rescues him from the band of poachers that kidnapped him. Eagirl doesn't have time to be not-okay. She has a forest to protect. "I'm okay," I say again.

"I'm okay," says Aaron. He's searching for another carrot stick, but he's eaten them all. He sighs and sits back in his chair. "I'm okay."

"The next piece of news is tough, but I want you to know that it's okay to be a little sad, or to need some time to yourself afterward to think about it." Mom makes the same tight-mouthed smile that Dad and Ranger Danger did. The bad-news smile. "Our budget is very different with your dad not working."

"Whoa, whoa," says Dad. "I'll be working. Just not for much money. Not just yet. But who knows what this part could lead to?"

Mom sighs and smiles a little at Dad. "Right. So, we do need to make some changes. Less spending. We're going to be a one-car family now. We were thinking about getting rid of the green car anyway, and then the tree fell on it. I guess it was meant to be. I called my old boss at the grocery store, and he offered me my old job. The one I had before your brother was born, remember? And we're going to move into an apartment."

What?

"An apartment near the grocery store. Which will be great, because I can just walk to work. I know this is a lot, and I know it's hard to—"

An apartment? Mom keeps talking, but I can't hear a word she's saying. My ears are buzzing like I'm deep underwater. I love our house. And our yard! With the Douglas squirrels and the deer. I love it. How am I going to fit my stuff into an apartment? Why couldn't Mom just keep being home? Why does Dad want to be Lyle, Lyle, Crocodile? Do crocodiles even talk? I can't remember anything about that book, except that the crocodile liked to take baths. Are we going to be poor?

My eyes fill up with hot tears. I can't even think of a relevant Eagirl issue. So much for this being a great summer.

"My milk!" says Aaron. He's tipped his straw cup again. "My milk my milk my milk my milk!"

4

Our real estate agent, Jenna Kapow, looks like a gymnast from the future. Her short blond hair is all spiked up on one side, and her suit is bright purple and blue. She has a crescent-moon earring in only one ear, and her eye shadow is electric green. I perch on the window seat in the dining room and listen to Jenna Kapow talk to Mom.

"This house sold *fast*," she says to Mom. They're sitting at the table. Mom is drinking coffee, and Jenna Kapow is drinking something green in a bottle she brought with her. "You're lucky the market is on your side right now. That great family just"—she snaps her fingers—"snapped it up! They've got those two kids, and this is *such* a great family home." She looks admiringly around the dining room.

I wrap my arms around myself. It *is* such a great family home. It's *my* family home. And now somebody else is going to live in it.

Jenna Kapow turns toward me. "Are you excited about your big move, Megan?"

Mom's already told her my name is Maggie. *I've* told her my name is Maggie. But she calls me Megan anyway.

"Not really," I say.

"This is all a pretty hard adjustment," Mom says to Jenna Kapow. "And with the house selling so quickly, Maggie really has only had a few weeks to come to terms with everything. But she's been a real trouper."

Mom smiles at me. I don't smile back.

Jenna Kapow sticks her bottom lip out at me.

"Aww, are you bummed? I bet you're a little bummed. But you know what, your new apartment is going to be super cozy. I hear you even get to share a room with your cute widdle brother!"

My stomach clenches up. I look at Mom. "I get to *what*?"

Mom sighs and gives Jenna Kapow a look. "I'm sorry, honey. I thought we told you, but everything's been so hectic and quick. It's a two-bedroom apartment. You and Aaron are going to share. But I think it'll be okay. I really do."

Jenna Kapow grimaces. "Whoops, sorry. Didn't mean to spill the beans. But you know what? When I was a kid, I didn't have any sisters or brothers, and I would have *loved* to share a room with one."

I glance at Mom, and she mouths the word *sorry* to me.

I wonder what she's sorry for. Totally turning my entire life upside down? Not telling me that I would have to share a room with Aaron? Hiring Jenna Kapow, the most annoying real estate agent in the state of Washington?

×××

After lunch, I pack up more of my room. I only get to bring four boxes of my stuff to the new apartment. *Four.* My bedding takes up one whole box, and that shouldn't even count as *my stuff* but Mom says it does. I considered not packing it, just to see what would happen, but with my recent luck, I'd have to sleep without a pillow for a month.

Mom stands in the doorway of my room with her arms crossed.

"If it's something only *you* use, it counts as *your* stuff."

"Really?" I point to the damp towel drying on the back of my desk chair. "I used that towel after my shower. I'll probably use it again all week. So does that count as *my* towel? Does it go in one of my personal boxes? Or—"

I stop when I see her face. She looks mad, but she also looks sad. And tired. And like she just wants me to stop talking, so I do.

"Are you almost finished packing?" Mom asks.

"Yeah," I say. I look around my room. I still have to sort through my books and decide which ones I'm keeping—Eagirl comics, books about kids surviving in the wilderness, books about people climbing mountains and exploring caves—and which ones I'm donating.

"Your dad and I need to sign some more papers, so we'll be in the dining room with Jenna. And hey, listen." She uncrosses her arms. "This is going to be okay. I know it's a pain, and a little scary and confusing, but it's going to be okay. Great, even."

"That's what I hear," I say.

"And don't leave damp towels on your wooden desk chair."

"Why?" I ask.

Mom looks like she's searching her brain for some information she can't find. "I don't actually know, but I know it's bad. Don't do it."

"Mmm, warping," says Jenna Kapow from somewhere in the hallway. "That'll cause warping. You don't want that. Your mom's right. It's bad. Don't do it."

I look at Mom. She shrugs and crinkles up her forehead like she's sorry Jenna Kapow is so awful. I shrug back.

Mom steps into the hallway and leans her head back like she's about to yell. "*Aa-ron*," she calls. Aaron is in the den watching TV. "Time to finish packing your stuff. Maggie will help you."

I sigh. I don't even want to pack my *own* stuff, never mind Aaron's.

Please, Mom mouths at me.

Aaron pads upstairs and down the hall to his bedroom.

Fine, I mouth back.

Aaron's room is a sleepy blue color. His shades are always half up, because that's the way he likes them. It makes the room a little darker, and that makes me feel like taking a nap. I yawn and sit down on his bed.

"Help you," Aaron says. He is standing in the middle of his floor with his palms up like he doesn't know where to start.

"Help *me*," I say. Sometimes Aaron gets *me* and *you* mixed up.

Aaron nods wisely and sits down next to me on the bed. "Help me. Help you."

I lean my head on Aaron's bony shoulder. We sit like that for a few seconds. He smells like his three-in-one apple shampoo, conditioner, and body wash.

"Are you mad that we're going to share a room?" I ask.

"No," says Aaron, looking at the wall across from us.

"Are you mad that we're not going to live in this house anymore?"

"No."

"Are you mad that you have to pack your stuff up and move it to an apartment all the way across town?"

Aaron pauses. "Help you," he says after a few seconds.

I sigh. "Okay, I'll help you. Come on."

We stand up and separate Aaron's things into four boxes. His bedding box, his book box, and his toy boxes. We work in silence, but when I look up at him, he's smiling gratefully at me. I don't want to share a room with anybody, but if I *have* to share a room with somebody, I'm glad it's going to be Aaron.

I wish I could go over to LaTanya's house—my second favorite house—and sit on her bedroom floor on her soft, pink carpet and tell her about everything that's happening. About Aaron, Dad's job, Mom's job, the move. But I can't, because she's not there. She's still in Vancouver. And every time I think about calling to talk to her, I get a weird feeling in my stomach and my face gets hot and my skin feels too tight. I'll tell her when she gets back. When I can go over to her house and sit on her floor and talk to her the way I always do. Then *some*thing will feel normal again.

5

The phone rings before I'm even awake. It's Moving Day. I'm groggy, and my mouth tastes like beef jerky. My mouth always tastes like beef jerky in the morning. I almost never even *eat* beef jerky. It's one of the great mysteries of the universe.

I open one eye and wait to hear if the phone's for me. There are footsteps, and then Mom knocks softly on my door. I know it's Mom, because Aaron never knocks softly. He pounds on the door and says, "I NEED TO COME IN!" Aaron hates when my door is closed. Dad never knocks softly, either. He knocks twice, loudly, and then says something like "Wakey, wakey, eggs and bakey." The soft knock is always Mom.

"Come in," I say. I sit up.

Mom opens the door. Her cell phone is lit up in her hand. Whenever I get a phone call, it's on Mom's phone, because I am the only twelve-year-old on the planet who doesn't have her own phone. I'm supposed to get my own phone when I turn fourteen, but now that Dad is going to be an actor practically for free and we're moving into an apartment, I don't know *what's* going to happen. I'll probably get an orange and a cornhusk doll like the girls in *Little House on the Prairie*. My stomach sinks a little.

"It's LaTanya, honey. Her family just got back from Vancouver. I know you've been missing her. We're going to start moving boxes to the apartment this morning, but she can join us there for dinner if you want! It'll be our first dinner in our new home."

My stomach sinks a *lot*. LaTanya doesn't know about the move yet. Or about Dad's job and *Lyle, Lyle, Crocodile*. Everything changed while she was on vacation.

"Great," I say, even though it isn't great. I take the phone from Mom, and she backs out of my room, closing the door.

"Mags, I miss you and I have to see you and I have *amazing* news." LaTanya sounds like she is jumping around her room. She's out of breath.

"Yay," I say, even though it doesn't *feel* yay. It feels like my life is getting ruined, and LaTanya's life is about to get amazing. Which is good for her. I'm super happy for her. I just wish *both* our lives could be getting amazing at the same time. I look at the V-E-R-Y-B-E-S-T bracelet on my wrist.

"Dad is going to be assistant head coach of the Seahawks!" she says.

I blink. It takes a second for me to understand exactly what that means. LaTanya's dad has been a coach in Canada for years. That's why she spends so much time in Vancouver. That means he and LaTanya's mom aren't rich, they're just regular. It means they live in a regular-sized house and buy regular amounts of stuff. It means he isn't famous or anything. We never see him coach football on TV.

"Wow," I say. "So he's going to coach...real football? During actual games?"

"Yes!" squeals LaTanya. She used to not like it when I called American football *real football*, but now that he's going to coach the Seahawks, I guess she doesn't mind. "He's going to coach here at home, and he's going to be on TV, and he's going to make *a million* dollars! *Aaaaah!*" she screams.

"Aaaah," I say.

"Mom says the first thing we're going to do is buy a big house with a big yard," says LaTanya.

Our new apartment doesn't have a yard. Mom showed me the virtual tour online. It has a small balcony that looks out over some gravel and a hill of invasive blackberry vines behind the building.

"Cool," I say.

"And Dad says I can *finally* get a puppy because we'll have more room for one!"

"Yay," I say. My new apartment doesn't allow pets.

It says so on the website. "I have to go, LaTanya. But I'm so happy for you! Tell your dad I said congratulations. It's going to be really cool to see him on TV."

"Well, that's another thing," says LaTanya. "We get to go to *all* the home games, which means I get to take *you* to some of them! And training camp is in a few weeks, and I get to take you to one of the practices. Aaron can come, too!"

Aaron loves watching football. He'd probably love going to one of the training-camp practices. But sometimes he gets upset when things are different than he's used to, or when we're out in public. He's been having a harder time with that lately.

I don't feel like telling LaTanya about Aaron's sensory stuff right now. I don't feel like telling her *anything* right now.

After we hang up, I head into the kitchen and hand Mom her phone. All of the cabinets and drawers are open and completely empty.

"Mr. Richards is going to coach the Seahawks now," I say. "He's assistant head coach." My voice doesn't sound happy or sad. It just sounds like a voice, like people on the news. They just tell information. They don't sound happy or sad about it.

"Oh, wow! That's amazing!" Mom puts her hands up to her pink face. She's been cleaning and moving boxes, and her hair is in two messy braids. "What incredible news, honey." She sighs and looks around. "I just wanted to do a last check in here. We don't want to leave anything behind!" Mom sticks the phone in her back pocket. She looks hopeful and happy, like this won't be so bad. I feel awful for being as mopey as I've been over the last few weeks. Eagirl wouldn't mope. She would fix everything.

I wrap my arms around Mom's waist and squeeze. She squeezes me back.

"I know this is a lot," she says. "But you are handling all of these changes *so* well."

I don't think I am handling *anything* well. But maybe Mom's been too busy to notice. And maybe that's good. She needs somebody solid to count on. She needs someone who is up for a challenge.

"Oh! Is LaTanya coming for dinner?" Mom asks.

I bite the inside of my cheek. "Actually, I forgot to ask her," I say. "Can I use your phone again?"

I can be brave. I can tell LaTanya what's going on.

I take the phone and go back to my room. Well, my *old* room. I take a deep breath and close the door.

The problem is, there are two kinds of brave. There's the kind of brave that's like Eagirl breaking into an island prison in *The Exceptional Eagirl #12* to save Lawrence Nightingale, who was wrongfully imprisoned by a corrupt judge.

And then there's the kind of brave that means you have to listen to someone tell you how sorry they are for you. I don't feel that kind of brave, but I dial LaTanya's number anyway.

My new apartment stinks. It's on the second floor, and it's small, and it only has two bedrooms in it: the one Mom is going to share with Dad, and the one I am going to share with Aaron. Aaron takes for*ever* to fall asleep at night. At our house, Mom lies down in his bed with him until he's asleep, and it takes at least an hour.

I open the front door. "Mom," I yell down the stairs.

"Ungh-huh?" she yells from halfway up. She is carrying a big box marked KITCHEN STUFF.

"Are you going to be in my room all night, now that I have to share with Aaron? Or are you going to want *me* to lie down with him?"

Mom clomps up the top two stairs and sets down the box. She rubs her back. "Maggie, I don't know. I guess we'll see what happens. Okay?"

I don't really want Mom in my room while I'm reading

Eagirl comics or trying to fall asleep. It would be weird. I don't want Aaron in my room while I'm doing those things, either, but he will be.

"Ungh." Mom picks up the box again and shoulders past me into the kitchen.

"Can I help with anything?" I ask. I flex my biceps.

"Yes! You're supposed to be helping with your brother."

We both look over at Aaron. He's arranging the letter magnets on the fridge. We haven't unpacked the toilet paper or the towels yet, but we've unpacked the letter magnets. We've also unpacked the wooden kitchen signs Dad collects from defunct clam-chowder restaurants on the East Coast. They say things like: CHOWDER, CHOWDER, CHOWDER and HOT CLAM CHOWDER and SOUPS 'N CHOWDERS. Most people would wait to unpack their weird signs until the useful stuff is all unpacked. My parents' priorities are different than most people's priorities.

There are a million letter magnets on our fridge, because anytime one of them gets lost, Aaron freaks out and we have to buy a whole new set. A couple weeks ago, he was trying to arrange them in alphabetical order, but he couldn't find the E. So he said, *E E E E E E E please please please please please I need an E I need an E*, and now we have our fourth set of letter magnets. Some of the letters get lost easier than others. We always have a lot of L's and N's. We lose E's pretty easily, though.

Aaron seems fine with his letters, so when Mom goes back outside to bring up another box, I go to my room.

Which I guess is technically *our* room.

Our room is the color of mushroom soup. Our new bunk bed is against one wall, and my desk is against the window. There are six unopened boxes on the floor. That's most of the stuff Aaron and I were allowed to take with us.

I didn't get to take *all* of my stuff, because it wouldn't all fit in here with Aaron's stuff, too. Dad told me to think of it as a good opportunity to decide what's really important to me. What's really important to me is having my own room and some privacy, but I didn't tell him that. It would have hurt his feelings.

I tear the tape off a box marked MAGGIE'S ROOM STUFF. I pull out Anderson Cooper: a stuffed rabbit my mom bought when she was pregnant with me. His name is Anderson Cooper because I heard that name on TV when I was really little, and I thought it sounded like a nice name for my rabbit. I throw Anderson Cooper onto the top bunk and make a mental note to hide him under my bedding when that box makes it up the stairs. Aaron tries to steal Anderson Cooper whenever he finds him, and now it's going to be a lot harder to keep him hidden.

A picture frame with a picture of me and LaTanya is

in the box, too. I take it out and set it up on my desk. I like this picture. It's from when everything was fine and normal. Dad wasn't an unemployed actor, and Aaron was just a baby. LaTanya didn't have a million dollars or a puppy, and I didn't live in a tiny apartment that smells weird, like there's a garbage dumpster right outside my bedroom window. Which there is.

"Knock, knock!" Dad says, even though my door's open and he isn't actually knocking. He's standing in the hallway with a box marked AARON'S BEDDING. "Can I come in?"

"Yep," I say.

He sets the box on the bottom bunk mattress and sits down next to it.

"This isn't such a bad little apartment," he says.

"It smells a little weird," I say, but I nod a little like I mostly agree with him. "Kind of like wet trash."

"That's the smell of nature! Look at all those blackberry bushes you can see from your window." Dad gets up and opens the window behind my desk. A breeze wafts the garbage smell right to my nose.

"I think it's the smell of the dumpster. It's right under my bedroom window," I say. "And did you know those blackberry bushes are really bad for Washington? They're invasive, and they choke out the plants that are actually supposed to be here." I know a lot about the plants of Washington.

When I'm a forest ranger, I can save campers from bears and stop babies from eating poison ivy. Just like Eagirl.

"Well, the blackberry flowers are pretty," says Dad. He takes a last look out the window. "I'd better get back to helping your mom bring boxes in. It's kind of cool being on the second floor, isn't it? It's like living in a tree house or something."

"Sure," I say.

"Finish unpacking so you can show LaTanya your new room! It'll be great to see her for dinner. You two have a lot of catching up to do! I saw her dad on the news last night. Pretty exciting stuff. Go, Hawks!"

"Go, Hawks," I say.

"Oh! I won't be able to hang around long after dinner." Dad leans against my doorjamb. "My big *Lyle* callback is tonight! Wish me a broken leg!" He wiggles his eyebrows.

"Break a leg," I say.

I wish I could be excited about Dad's callback, but I'm not. And I don't want to show LaTanya my new room. It's smaller than my old room, *and* I'm sharing it with Aaron. I don't really want to show her my new apartment at all, but it would be a hard thing to hide. Maybe when she gets her new, big house we can just hang out there all the time, and she'll forget about my little trash-smelling apartment.

"*Aaaaaahhh!*" screams Aaron. I race to the kitchen. He's

lying on his side, trying to look under the fridge.

"What letter did you drop down there, buddy?" I ask.

"S S S S S S I drop my S I drop my S," says Aaron.

I get down next to him and try to look under the fridge, but it's too dark. I can't see anything.

I look around the kitchen. There are four big boxes lined up on the counter, and they're all marked KITCHEN STUFF. There's a bigger box on the floor marked HANDY STUFF (KITCHEN? BATHROOM?). I peel the tape off the top of that one and open it up. There's a flashlight right on top. *My lucky day*, I think, and then I almost laugh, because actually, it's the opposite of my lucky day.

I turn on the flashlight and get back down on the floor next to Aaron. I shine the light under the fridge. Aaron and I scream at the same time.

"MY S!" screams Aaron. "MY S!"

"AAAAHHH!" I scream.

Right next to Aaron's S magnet, there is a bloated old diaper wrapped up into the shape of a football.

I hear two sets of feet running up the stairs outside, and then the front door opens. Mom and Dad rush into the kitchen.

"What's going on?" Mom says. "We heard you guys screaming all the way down in the parking lot!"

"Are you both okay?" asks Dad.

"No, we're not okay," I say. I stand up and brush off my pants. "We found a dirty diaper under the fridge! That's *disgusting*!"

"Gross," says Dad. He gets down and looks under the fridge with the flashlight. "I'll get that out with a hanger. Don't worry."

"Don't *worry*? What else could be lurking in this apartment? Dead rats? A jar of earwax?" I'm shaking.

"I wonder where we packed the hangers," says Dad.

"Why would there be a jar of earwax?" asks Mom.

"I don't know, Mom! Why is there a dirty diaper?" My face feels hot. I want to go lie down in my room, except I can't, because I don't know where the box with my bedding is.

"Why don't you go back to unpacking your room," says Dad. "We'll handle the diaper and the S. You read an Eagirl comic or something, and just relax."

"Fine," I say. I don't know where my bedding is, but I know where Aaron's bedding is.

Back in our room, I unpack the box of Aaron's sheets and blankets. I make the bottom bunk and tuck his big plastic train next to his stuffed elephant. Those are the things Aaron likes to sleep with at night. I dig *The Exceptional Eagirl #45* out of a box marked MAGGIE'S BOOKS and lie down next to the train and the elephant.

In #45, Eagirl's nest has been completely destroyed.

Her furniture is smashed, and her computers and crime-fighting technology are missing. She has to move in with Possum Sauce for a while, until they figure out who wrecked Eagirl's nest and why.

Possum Sauce tries to be a good hostess, but she's kind of messy, and Eagirl isn't. Possum Sauce is up all night, painting, snacking, and developing technology to track villains. Eagirl gets up at the crack of dawn, eats a protein-rich breakfast, and does forty-five minutes of intense exercise designed to help her defeat villains three times her size. They keep waking each other up and getting on each other's nerves. It isn't the best situation, but by the end of #45, they realize they need to focus on the things that make them a great team, and they solve the mystery of Eagirl's wrecked nest together.

This is kind of like that. I don't want to live in this crappy apartment, but I have to. So, I guess I might as well try to focus on being a team player. Even if I have to share a room with my brother, and the whole place smells like trash, and there are dirty diapers under the fridge.

7

"I can't believe you moved!" squeals LaTanya. Her arms are still wrapped around me, and we're kind of rocking back and forth. We're both still wearing our V-E-R-Y-B-E-S-T bracelets. "I was only gone for a month!"

"Yeah, well," I say. "I guess a lot can happen in a month."

LaTanya looks the same, but different. I think her braids are shinier than they used to be. Her pink tank top with pineapples all over it seems more expensive, too, even though I know I saw her wear it before she was rich. I wish I'd at least brushed my hair this morning, but I packed up my hairbrush yesterday and forgot which box it was in.

We sit down at the table. The table isn't exactly in the kitchen, and it isn't in the living room, either. It's kind of in between. Everything except the bedrooms and bathroom are just one big room in the new apartment. I miss having a dining room with its own walls.

"Pizza is on the way," I say. "I got pepperoni and pine-apple just for you."

I like calling the pizza place, because it makes me feel at least five years older than I am. And when I'm five years older, I'll be allowed to wear makeup and have my own phone. And I probably won't be living in this apartment anymore. Maybe Dad will be a famous actor. If a lot can happen in a month, a *ton* can happen in five years. We'll probably be living on Mars.

"And you're moving, too," I say, even though I don't want to talk about it.

"I know! I can't wait. My dad says we're staying in Renton, because that's where the Seahawks practice anyway. And that way I can stay at the same school."

I feel a little relieved. I would hate to be at a different school than LaTanya.

"And plus," says LaTanya, "we can get a *massive* house in Renton for the price of just a regular big house on Mercer Island or somewhere fancy. My mom says we're going to put in an in-ground pool and a juice bar."

"Great," I say. It doesn't really sound that great, though. There's no pool at my new apartment. And there's not even juice in our *fridge*. There's just milk and a bag of apples, so far.

Aaron strolls into the dining-room-that's-not-a-room.

"Aaahh!" He says. "There's a dirty diaper under the fridge!" He cracks up like he just said the funniest thing in the world.

"Ew, what?" says LaTanya.

"I have no idea," I say. "He just says stuff."

LaTanya nods. "Little kids are weird."

My stomach gets tight and my cheeks get hot. "He's not weird. He's *autistic*. Remember?"

LaTanya's eyes get bigger. "Oh! No, I know. I didn't mean *he's* weird. I just meant, like, *all* little kids are weird."

I nod and look at the table. Little kids *are* weird. But I don't want anyone calling Aaron weird. Aaron isn't weird. Aaron's the most normal part of my life right now.

"So, you said he's starting his therapies soon. They're going to help him with stuff?"

I straighten up. "Yeah. And so will I."

"You're such an awesome sister. I bet that's why you have to share a room with him. So you can help him out," says LaTanya.

I hadn't thought of it like that. I bet that *is* why I have to share a room with him. Mom and Dad are so smart. *I* thought we had to get a two-bedroom apartment because we don't have much money anymore, but maybe it's also a little because Mom and Dad know Aaron needs someone to help him and guide him through life, and they knew I'd be the exact perfect person to do it. His big sister. His hero. I take a deep breath. It doesn't smell that much like wet garbage anymore.

Mom's cell phone rings on the counter. I jump up and look at the number on the screen. "Mom!" I yell. "Pizza's here!" I press the green button on the screen and hold the phone up to my ear. "Hello?"

"Hey, uh, I'm downstairs with your pizza," says the voice on the phone. "You gotta come get it."

I look down at my bare feet. "Why do I have to come down and get it? When we lived in our house, you guys used to just bring it to the front door."

"There's a coupla guys moving a reclining chair down the stairs, and I couldn't squeeze by. I'm a big fella. You want your pizza, you're going to have to come down here yourself."

"Great," I say, but I don't actually mean great. I press the red button. "Mom!" I yell again. "The pizza guy says he won't come up here, so you have to go downstairs and get it."

Mom appears in the dining-room-that's-not-a-room. "Okeydoke," she says. "Your dad's getting dressed for his big callback tonight, so keep an eye on Aaron for a sec. I'll be right back."

"Aaahh!" says Aaron. "There's a dirty diaper under the fridge!"

"Not anymore, buddy," says Mom. "We threw it away." She closes the door behind her.

✖✖✖

At dinner, Mom and Dad ask LaTanya a million questions about her dad and his new job with the Seahawks. I think about other things instead. Like about how I'm going to help Aaron. It'll be like *The Exceptional Eagirl #4*, when Eagirl finds Rex, the orphaned baby red-tailed hawk.

"Here, Aaron," I say. "There's only one slice of pepperoni left. I know it's your favorite. It's all yours." I drop the slice onto Aaron's plate and smile down at him, like Eagirl smiled at Rex, the red-tailed hawk.

"I'm all done," says Aaron. He pushes the plate away, gets up from the table, and goes to our room.

Fine.

"Your dad is a local celebrity anyway," says Dad. "Renton is going to be so happy to get him back! He was the star of our football team when we were in high school, you know. He could have played for the Seahawks, if he hadn't gotten injured in college."

"Yeah, everybody's really excited. They're doing a story on him in the *Renton Reporter*, and he's getting paid to do commercials! He just got a car commercial for

Renton Mazda and an appliance commercial for Duke and Kitty's Refrigeration," says LaTanya.

"Cars and refrigeration! That's terrific! You know, I don't know if Maggie told you yet, but I've got a callback for an acting job this evening." Dad is beaming at LaTanya.

I push my chair away from the table. "LaTanya, let's go out on the balcony and look at the, uh, blackberry vines."

"No, she didn't! What's your callback for?" LaTanya asks Dad.

"It's a web series! A modern retelling of *Lyle, Lyle, Crocodile*. Can you guess which part I've been called back for?" Dad grins like we haven't already had this same conversation.

"What's a web series?" asks LaTanya.

That's what I said. "So, balcony?" I ask. "Or do you want to go to my room? It's kind of small, and Aaron's in there, too, but—"

"It's an online series! A show! Hang on," says Dad. He gets up from the table and disappears down the hall.

"He's so excited about this callback," says Mom. Her cheeks are pink, and she's smiling at LaTanya. "And I couldn't be prouder. I imagine your mom must feel the same way about your dad right now!"

I slide down in my chair. There is a big difference between my dad's callback and LaTanya's dad's million-dollar Seahawks contract. Why does my mom have to say the most embarrassing things I could possibly imagine?

LaTanya nods at Mom, chewing her pizza. "It's important to have dreams. My mom says without dreams, nobody has much."

"That is exactly right," says Dad, coming back to the table with his voice muffled underneath his big, green, fake-looking crocodile snout. "Your mom is a smart lady."

"Whoa," says LaTanya. "That's really—"

"It's really something, isn't it?" says Dad. "I made it myself. I wanted to show them how committed I am to the role. Speaking of which, I want to get to the callback early, so I'm going to head into Seattle now." Dad crosses his fingers and shakes them at us. "Here goes nothin'!"

Mom gets up and wraps Dad in a big hug. She kisses him on the cheek for an embarrassing amount of time. He can't kiss her back because of his green crocodile snout. "Break a leg!"

"Well," I say once the door closes, "what do you want to—"

"Actually, my mom's going to pick me up in a few minutes because we have to get up early to go house-shopping tomorrow." LaTanya looks sorry. "Let me know what happens with your dad's callback!"

"Yeah, okay," I say.

It still smells like dumpster trash, but the blackberry vines do look kind of pretty at night outside my window. The flowers are small and white, and the hill of vines looks like a place fairies would live, if fairies were real. I finish making my bed and get ready to crawl in with the Eagirl comic I started reading earlier this afternoon. But then I remember that I'd thrown Anderson Cooper up onto my mattress to keep him away from Aaron. And he wasn't there when I put my sheets and blankets on.

I hang my head down over the rail on the side of my bunk to look at Aaron. He's already asleep. I guess he didn't need Mom to lie with him tonight after all. I guess I'm enough. His big sister. His hero.

Aaron's eyelashes flutter a little on his pink cheeks, and he lets out a long, quiet sigh. Anderson Cooper is tucked in the crook of his elbow.

8

On Monday morning, while Aaron and I eat our cereal, Dad is practically dancing in front of the single-cup coffee maker. His callback went well. He hasn't heard from the director yet, but she's supposed to call before noon. When the coffee maker stops gurgling, Dad removes Mom's HAPPY MOTHER'S DAY mug and stirs in milk and a sweetener, still dancing. And now humming. He places it at her spot on the table.

Mom appears in the kitchen and sinks down in her chair, breathing in the smell of her coffee.

"Are you ready for your first day?" Dad asks her. "It's your mom's first day, you know," he says, looking at me.

"Yay," I say, because I don't know what else to say. She's managing the grocery store. Well, assistant managing.

"I hope I'm ready," says Mom. She takes a long sip. "And tomorrow is *Aaron's* first day of OT and speech." She squeezes Dad's arm. "And *your* first day as chauffeur!"

"Yay," I say again. "What's OT?"

"Occupational therapy," says Dad.

"What? For Aaron? Aaron doesn't have an occupation. He's four," I say.

Aaron doesn't say anything. He's busy eating his cereal.

"Honestly, I'm not entirely sure what it is myself. I guess we'll find out together," Dad says.

Dad's phone buzzes on the counter. He picks it up, looks at the number, and dashes down the hallway. Nobody interesting ever calls Dad, so we know who this is. Mom bites her bottom lip and wrinkles her forehead at me. I shrug at her. If Dad gets the part, he plays a giant crocodile in a web series that nobody I know has ever heard of. If he doesn't get the part, he *doesn't* play a giant crocodile in a web series. I like when Dad's happy, and I guess getting the part would make him happy, so that's really the only thing tipping the scale for me.

"*Unbelievable,*" shouts Dad from my parents' bedroom. "*Holy Toledo! Stellar! Yes!*"

So, I guess my dad is a web-series actor now. Great.

✗✗✗

By 3:00 p.m., I am more bored than I've ever been in my life. LaTanya was supposed to call so we could make plans. But at 12:15 p.m. I realized that LaTanya only has

Mom's phone number. And Mom's phone is with Mom at her new grocery store job. And I don't know LaTanya's number, because I just press LATANYA RICHARDS on my Mom's contact list when I want to call her. So, I'm lying on my bed with Anderson Cooper, watching Aaron spread out his sight-word cards into the shape of a perfect square in the middle of our floor.

"Aaron," I say. "How do you spell 'that'?"

"T-H-A-T spells 'THAT,'" says Aaron.

"Yeah! How do you spell 'WILL'?"

"W-I-L-L spells 'WILL,'" says Aaron.

Aaron can spell any sight word. He gets new packs of them and learns all of the words immediately.

"Aaron," I say. "How do you spell 'CROCODILE'?"

Aaron looks up at me. "No," he says.

"Yeah," I say. "I don't like crocodiles that much, either."

Aaron shakes his head and gathers his sight-word cards into a stack again.

I roll over on my back and toss Anderson Cooper up to the ceiling. It's probably ten degrees hotter on the top bunk than it is on the bottom bunk. And our new apartment doesn't have air-conditioning. The window is open, but the breeze is more a vehicle for the dumpster stink than it is for cooling.

Dad pokes his head inside our room.

"This is nice, isn't it?" he says. "Just hanging out in your room together. Two kids on summer break."

"Yeah," I say. "Hey, what's going to happen to me tomorrow? When you and Aaron are at therapy and Mom's at work? And now you're doing rehearsals and taping in Seattle a bunch of nights a week. Am I just going to go with you to therapy? Or am I going to be alone all summer? And who's going to make dinner?" I sit up.

"Hey, you know, those are good questions, kiddo," says Dad. He scratches his chin. "Your mom and I talked about this stuff, and we'll run our idea by you when she gets home."

I narrow my eyes. "Why can't you just tell me now?"

Then I unnarrow my eyes. Maybe he can't tell me now because it's a *surprise*. Maybe I won't be alone all summer long. Maybe I'll get to go to a really amazing summer camp for the rest of the summer. Maybe it's Junior Forest Ranger Camp, which I've been dying to go to practically my entire life, where you learn how to tie knots and start fires using two sticks and rescue wildlife. I've left Junior Forest Ranger Camp pamphlets out for my parents to find every time I get one in the mail. Which is a lot, because all of my Eagirl comics come with postcards stuck inside that you can fill out and send away for Junior Forest Ranger Camp pamphlets. And I always fill them out. This could be the best summer *ever*.

"We'll tell you tonight," says Dad.

When Mom gets home, I am desperate to find out what the surprise is. And I'm *also* desperate to talk to LaTanya and tell her that I'm going to Junior Forest Ranger Camp, after I find out for sure that I definitely am. I even feel a little better about moving to this apartment and LaTanya becoming a millionaire and probably buying a mansion, because I'll be a Junior Forest Ranger, and that makes up for everything.

"Mom!" I pull her inside and lead her over to the couch. I plop us both down. "How was your first day at work? And did LaTanya call me? And Dad says you guys have a big surprise for me. Can you tell me what it is? Does it start with a J? Am I going to love it?"

Mom puts her hands over her eyes and lies back. "Maggie. I'm going to need a minute here. I've had a very long day."

"Yeah, I bet. Only, I've *also* had a very long day, and it was mostly because I didn't have LaTanya to talk to or hang out with, because you took your phone to work and I didn't have LaTanya's number, and it's *hot* in this apartment because there's no AC, and—"

"Maggie." Mom takes her hands off her eyes and looks at me. "I need. A minute."

Fine.

I go to my room to find Aaron. He's sitting at my desk, writing out a list of words.

CAN
HOW
GET
WORK
MICE
CAT
WILL

"Good spelling, Aaron," I say.
"How do you spell 'CROCODILE'?" asks Aaron.
"C-R-O-C-O-D-I-L-E," I say.
"C-R-O-C-O-D-I-L-E," Aaron says. Then he writes it down at the bottom of his list of words.

CROCODILE

I ruffle Aaron's hair and climb the ladder to my bed. I look under my blanket for Anderson Cooper, but he's not there. I hang my head over the rail again. There are Aaron's plastic train, stuffed elephant, and Anderson Cooper, all resting in a cozy line on Aaron's pillow.
Fine.

I probably won't want to take Anderson Cooper to Junior Forest Ranger Camp anyway. Forest rangers don't sleep with old stuffed rabbits. They save *real* rabbits from wildfires. Kind of like Eagirl in almost every *Exceptional Eagirl* comic. Saving the forest and her friends from all kinds of devastation.

I sigh and lie back on my pillow. I can't *wait* to go to Junior Forest Ranger Camp.

I'm not going to Junior Forest Ranger Camp. That wasn't the surprise my parents had for me. The surprise they had was almost identical to the awful surprise they had the last time I thought they were surprising me with something good.

It's probably good that I'm not going to Junior Forest Ranger Camp. I would make a terrible junior forest ranger anyway. I obviously have terrible instincts and recall. If I were cut out for it, I might have remembered that my parents once surprised me with a birthday visit from Grandma Barrel, who thinks I'm too old to read comic books.

This time, it's worse than a birthday visit from Grandma Barrel. It's an entire month-long visit from Grandma Barrel. A month of Grandma Barrel sleeping on the couch. In our very small apartment.

Tuesday morning, Mom sits down in her chair at the table and yawns. "I'll have a double," she calls to Dad, who is dancing again at the coffee maker.

"You got it, boss," says Dad, all cheery.

"I'll have a single," I say. I don't drink coffee, but I want to. Eagirl drinks coffee. So does Ranger Danger. And so do *real* forest rangers. Unlike with makeup and cell phones, my parents have never decided on an official start date for my coffee consumption.

"I don't think so. Not today, Maggie," says Mom. She yawns again.

"Why *not* today?" I ask.

No one says anything for a minute. The coffee maker gurgles the end of Mom's double. Dad stirs in the milk and sweetener. He brings the mug to the table and sets it in front of Mom, and then he leans down and whispers something in her ear. Mom looks at Dad and shrugs.

"Yeah, okay," says Mom. "We can't think of a reason why not today. How do you want your coffee?"

"*Woo-hoo!*" I punch the air like I just *finally* scored a point in an entire game of losing bad and scoring nothing. *Maybe* a tree crushed our car, and *maybe* we had to move to a crappy little apartment because we don't have much money anymore, and *maybe* my dad lost his job and is a part-time crocodile, and *maybe* my mom's going to be cranky and tired every day because she has to work in a grocery store so we can pay bills, and *maybe* my best friend just basically won the lottery of life and her dad is going to be a superstar millionaire and they're going to live in a mansion with a new puppy, but *I get to drink coffee now*. That's *something*. "Black," I say. "I'll take it black." Black is how Eagirl drinks her coffee, and it's how forest rangers drink their coffee, too. I'm going to be a drinker of black coffee.

Dad makes me a cup of coffee in a blue mug that says PNW: Where Adventure Finds You. PNW stands for Pacific Northwest, which is the part of the country Washington is in. Exactly zero adventures have ever found me here, no matter how many times Dad tries to convince me that living in an apartment is an adventure. But maybe someday. I hope. I like the mug anyway. It has a pine tree painted inside on the bottom.

Dad puts the coffee in front of me, and I close my eyes and get a good whiff of my first cup, just like the people wearing bathrobes do in coffee commercials. It smells strong. It smells like it'll taste good.

Which is why I am very surprised when it doesn't taste good at *all*. It tastes like burnt dirt. I swallow.

"What do you think?" asks Mom.

"Do we have another coffee drinker in the house?" asks Dad.

"We don't live in a house anymore," I say. I look down into the coffee. It's so dark I can't see the pine tree at the bottom. "We live in an apartment."

xxx

I copy LaTanya's number into Dad's phone before Mom leaves for work. When Aaron and Dad sit down on the couch to watch *Super Why!* on TV, I take his phone to my room and close the door.

"Hello?" says LaTanya.

Another unfair thing is that even when LaTanya *wasn't* rich, she always had her own phone. Everyone has their own phone. Except me.

"Hi! It's Maggie. On my dad's phone." I say. "Did you find a house yesterday?"

"Yeah, we did! I tried calling you a million times to tell you, but nobody answered."

"My mom took her phone to work," I say. "She said to tell you to call my dad's number now."

"Oh, okay. We put in an offer on a house, and they accepted it right away because they're big Seahawks fans!"

"That's great," I say. I sit down at my desk. "Is it big?"

"It's *so* big! And there's a movie theater inside! It's got big movie-chair seats and a movie screen and everything!"

"That's great," I say again. I tear a little strip off the side of a piece of paper and roll it up into a tiny little ball.

"And there's a huge fenced-in yard, and it's perfect for a dog. My dad wants a big dog, but my mom wants a really tiny one so she can take it places in her purse. I don't care what kind of dog we get, as long as they let me name it, which they will."

"Great," I say. I rip off another strip of paper and roll it up.

"There are *two* kitchens in this house! One is like the main kitchen downstairs, and then the other one is outside the movie theater, which is right next to my bedroom. And my bedroom is *so big*! The closet is the same size as my entire old room!"

"Wow," I say. *Riiiip*, roll.

"And there's an arcade room! The old owners said they're going to leave all the old arcade games because they're old and want to move to a smaller place and they don't want to take all their stuff with them. It's so fun! There's even a claw machine."

"Great!" *Riiiiip*, roll.

"Can you come over to my old house today? You don't have to help me pack or anything. My dad's paying a company to move us, and they'll pack up so we don't have to."

"Cool." *Riiiip*, roll. "I can't, though. It's Aaron's first day of therapy, so I want to go and be supportive and hang out with my dad." Actually, I was planning to ask LaTanya if she wanted to hang out today, and I don't really want to hang out with my dad while we wait around for Aaron. But I also don't want to hear all about how great LaTanya's new house is, either.

After I hang up the phone, I stay in my desk chair, ripping and rolling strips from that piece of paper.

"Run to your room and get your shoes, buddy," Dad yells from somewhere in the apartment. "It's almost time to leave for your first OT session!"

I hear Aaron's shoeless feet pad down the hallway. He appears in the doorway and looks around the room for his shoes.

"Hi, buddy," I say. "Your shoes are over here by the win—"

"*My list!*" Aaron yells. He is staring at the desk with a red little face full of rage. "My list! You ripped my list! You ripped my list!"

I look down at what's left of the paper I'm shredding and turn it over. It's Aaron's list of words.

"My list!" Tears are streaming down Aaron's cheeks, now. "You ripped my list!" His fists are balled up at his sides. His mouth is a perfect frown.

Dad pokes his head in our room. "What's going on?" His eyes get wider when he sees Aaron looking like a caricature of an upset person.

"I'm sorry," I say, looking from Aaron to Dad. "I didn't know it was his list. I thought it was just a piece of paper."

"You ripped my list," sniffs Aaron. He turns around and buries his face in Dad's shirt. Dad rubs his hair and makes shushing sounds to Aaron, but he is giving me an extremely disappointed look.

"I don't understand why you would rip up a piece of paper without checking to see if anything was on it," he says.

"Why *would* I check to see if anything was on it?" I felt bad for Aaron, but now I mostly feel bad for *me*. "You're mad at me because I ripped up a random piece of paper that appeared to be blank? That's not fair. And by the way, if I still had my own room, that piece of paper *would* have been blank, because it would be on my desk in *my* room, and I wouldn't have to share every single thing with Aaron!" My eyes feel hot and watery, but I will them not to cry.

"We need to go. Aaron, buddy, you can make a new list when we get back. Let's put your shoes on. Maggie, let's go." Dad turns away from me to help Aaron.

Sometimes life is very unfair, and I wish I'd get adopted by a family of eagles.

10

The therapy place is bright and noisy. There are a yellow couch and a bunch of red chairs for little kids. There are toys all over the place and a basket full of magazines and books. A big poster on the wall has a cartoon owl making the *shh* sign and wearing headphones. Under the owl, it says *Please be quiet for our sound-sensitive friends*. Most of the kids in the waiting room are not being quiet at all. A little boy with red hair keeps furiously crashing toy cars into the leg of a chair. A little girl is howling with her face buried in her mom's leg, and another kid is covering his ears, complaining loudly to his dad about the noise. I guess he's one of the *sound-sensitive friends* from the poster.

"Keep an eye on Aaron. I need to fill out some paperwork at the desk." Dad walks away, and Aaron looks at me with huge eyes. I reach down and squeeze his hand.

"You're going to have fun, Aaron," I say. Aaron doesn't

look like he believes me, and I don't blame him. *I* don't believe me. Aaron sometimes doesn't like new stuff, and therapy is *all* new stuff.

The little girl has stopped crying, and she looks over at Aaron, wiping her nose on her sleeve.

"Hi," I say to her. I nudge Aaron. "Say hi, Aaron."

Aaron just keeps looking at me.

"This is Aaron," I say to the little girl.

"I know that," says the little girl. "You said his name a bunch of times already." She comes closer, and her mom politely waves at us before picking up a magazine.

"Oh," I say. "Well, what's your name?"

"Eva," says the girl.

"Eva! That's a nice name."

"I know that," Eva says again.

"Oh," I say. I wonder what Eva's deal is. I wonder why she's here. "Do you go to therapy too?" I ask.

Eva ignores my question. She narrows her eyes at Aaron. "Don't get therapy with Miss Jessica. She makes you put your hand in goop. I hate goop."

Aaron smiles a tiny smile at Eva. "I like goop," he says.

He does like goop. Mom has a different slime recipe for every holiday, and Aaron loves them all.

"I hate goop," says Eva.

Aaron and Eva stand there just looking at each other for

a minute. This is going well. Maybe Eva will be Aaron's first friend. Maybe we can set up playdates together, and I can be kind of the babysitter and entertainment director, and we can do crafts and nature walks.

But Eva's face doesn't look curious and calm anymore. It looks furious. Her fists are balled up at her sides, and she is shaking.

"I. Hate. Goop."

Her mom puts the magazine down. "Eva? Are you okay?"

"*I. Hate. Goop.*"

"Um," I say to Eva's mom. "I think she got upset because Aaron said he likes goop."

"Ohh," says Eva's mom. "Eva hates goop." She picks up the magazine again.

I look around for something to distract Aaron and get him away from this girl. I spot a big wooden cube with movable alphabet tiles. "Aaron, look over there! A cool alphabet toy!"

But Aaron doesn't look over there. He is looking at Eva, who is still freaking out about goop.

"I hate goop!" says Eva.

"I love goop!" says Aaron. He smiles at her. He wiggles the fingers of his right hand in front of his eyes. That's what he does when he's really happy.

"I HATE GOOP," says Eva.

"I *love* goop!" says Aaron.

None of the adults in the room seem to care what's going on. Dad is still at the front desk, and Eva's mom is engrossed in an article in her magazine. I guess it's up to me to get Aaron out of the situation before he gets punched. "Hey, guys," I say. "Why don't we forget about goop for a minute. Aaron, do you want to read a book with me?"

"No," says Aaron. "I want to play with *goop*!" He wiggles his fingers again.

"I HATE GOOP!" says Eva.

"I love goop!" says Aaron.

"Let's build a tower with some blocks," I say to Aaron. I try to wedge my body between Aaron and Eva.

Eva pushes me.

I fall against one of the red chairs.

Crack.

One of the chair legs is bent where it connects to the seat. Everyone in the waiting room is looking at me.

"I, um." I try to keep my voice from shaking. "I'm okay. This little girl pushed me, but it's fine. I'm fine." I stand up and adjust my shirt. My elbow hurts.

"Eva, did you push this girl?" asks Eva's mom. She puts the magazine down.

"Yes," says Eva. "She bumped me away from my friend."

"Did you bump her away from her friend?" Eva's mom looks at me.

"No!" I say. "I mean, I tried to get between her and my brother, because they were just getting each other upset." I try to make my voice calm and sensible, like a forest ranger. Like Eagirl. "I was only trying to help."

"Well, Eva doesn't like to be bumped." Eva's mom picks her magazine up again.

I rub my elbow.

"Aaron Chowder?" A woman in a pink sweat suit opens the door that leads to the therapy rooms and looks around for Aaron.

"I *hate* you, Miss Jessica," says Eva. "I hate you, and I hate goop."

The woman in the sweat suit looks at Eva with a fond smile. "I'll see you in about an hour, Eva! After Miss Susan! First, I've got a new little guy that I'm excited to meet. Aaron?"

Aaron crinkles his forehead at me.

Dad hurries over to us from the front desk. "Hey, buddy, are you ready to go in with Miss Jessica? Don't worry, we're coming with you today."

"I want a playdate with Aaron," says Eva.

"Great!" says Dad. "Maggie, why don't you give Eva's mom our information, then you can join us for Aaron's OT."

"I don't think that's—"

"Great idea!" says Eva's mom. She pulls out her phone. "What's your number, honey?"

I sit down on the couch next to Eva's mom. I give her Dad's cell phone number.

Eva sits down next to me.

"I hate goop," she says.

✖✖✖

When I join Dad and Aaron in Miss Jessica's therapy room, everybody is sitting on the floor. Miss Jessica is helping Aaron pour glitter through a funnel into an empty plastic bottle.

"Welcome, big sister," Miss Jessica says, motioning for me to sit on the floor.

I sink down next to Dad, across from Aaron.

"We're making a calming sensory bottle," says Miss Jessica. She waves her hand over a tray of beads, cut-up bits of pipe cleaner, and sequins. "Aaron will add some of these to the bottle, then we'll fill it with water and glycerin, and seal it up. It acts like a snow globe. Aaron can turn it upside down and watch it all float to the bottom when he's overwhelmed or upset."

It's actually kind of relaxing watching Aaron add sequins, beads with letters on them, and pipe cleaner pieces to his bottle. Until he accidentally knocks it over, and some of the glitter and beads spill out onto the carpet.

"No!" shrieks Aaron. "I spilled my bottle! My bottle my bottle my bottle my—"

Miss Jessica reaches for Aaron's spilled bottle and stands it up on the floor. "There, it's okay, Aaron. We'll just try that again!"

"I spilled my bottle," Aaron says sadly, looking at the contents that are still on the floor.

"Do you know what you can do when you're feeling frustrated?" Miss Jessica takes a deep breath and lets it out. "You can breathe just like that, or you can count to ten, very slowly. One, two, three…"

Aaron closes his eyes. "Four, five, six…"

"Seven, eight, nine, ten," we all say together.

OT isn't so bad, and neither is Miss Jessica.

11

"Hey, Mags, would you fetch my new snout?" Dad yells from the bathroom. He is in there covering his face in green face paint. "I left it on my bed."

Tonight is Dad's first *Lyle, Lyle, Crocodile* rehearsal.

"Why do you need to paint your face if it's just a rehearsal?" I hand him the snout.

"Because we're shooting promotional photos tonight, too." Dad fits his snout over his nose and mouth. This one at least looks like it wasn't made by a toddler. He steps back and looks at himself in the mirror. He is wearing a green spandex one-piece suit and a green bald cap. He looks like a nude half-alligator half-man. I shiver. His costume is very disturbing.

"How do I look?" he asks.

"Like a crocodile," I say. Maybe the *Lyle, Lyle, Crocodile* web series is supposed to be scary.

"C-R-O-C-O-D-I-L-E," says Aaron, squeezing past me into the bathroom. He looks up at Dad. "Spells 'crocodile.'"

"You're right, buddy, it does." Dad ruffles Aaron's hair. "Are you going to watch my web series when it comes out?"

"No," says Aaron. "I'm going to watch *Diagnosis Murder*."

"Hey, that's right, Aaron! Grandma Barrel gets here tomorrow. You love to watch *Diagnosis Murder* with Grandma, huh?"

"I like goop," says Aaron.

My stomach clenches up like a fist. I almost forgot about Grandma Barrel. In less than twenty-four hours, she'll be casting a shadow over our whole apartment, like Hawkmare, Eagirl's most terrifying nemesis. The comics never actually show Hawkmare's face—just her menacing shadow. If they did show her face, I bet it would look like Grandma Barrel's.

Keys jingle outside the front door.

"I'm home, family!" Mom calls from the hallway. Dad, Aaron, and I rush out to meet her. "Look at you, honey!" Mom kisses Dad on his snout. "Are you ready for your big night?"

"I sure am," says Dad. "Do I look crocodiley enough?"

"You look exactly crocodiley enough."

"Then tag! You're it. I'll see you after rehearsal."

I hug Dad goodbye. His spandex suit feels itchy and slippery against my face. I shiver again.

When the door closes, Mom turns to face me and Aaron. "Okay, guys. We have some work to do to get this place ready for Grandma Barrel's visit. Aaron, pick up your toys in the living room. Maggie, I need you to scrub the bathroom." Mom pokes her head into the bathroom and flicks on the light. "Oh, jeez. There's green paint everywhere. Maggie, grab a roll of paper towels, some cleaning spray, and a trash bag."

"Why do *I* have to scrub Dad's crocodile paint off the bathroom walls?" I cross my arms. "Can't he do that when he gets home? Can't *you* do it?"

Mom's eyes get wide, and I wish I hadn't said that. "No, I can't." Her voice is quiet and slow. It's her scary voice, and she doesn't use it very often. "I spent all day dealing with customer complaints, a broken toilet in the men's room, an onion display that was completely rotten on the bottom, and an employee who showed up two hours late for his shift. So, *you* can clean the bathroom. I am going to sit down for five minutes and have a cup of tea with my shoes off. Then I will do the dishes and the floors and the fifty thousand other things that need to get done around here. Is that okay with you, Maggie Chowder?"

"Yes," I say.

Mom's phone rings. She pulls it out of her back pocket, looks at the display, and holds it out to me. "It's LaTanya.

Just don't forget about the bathroom."

I nod and take the phone into my room.

"Hi, LaTanya."

"Maggie! We got a puppy! You're gonna love him. His name is Glitter, and he's a dachshund."

"Aww," I say. "I can't wait to meet him."

"Maybe you can meet him on Sunday! We have extra tickets to a Seahawks training-camp practice that day, and my dad said I can bring you and Aaron!"

Aaron likes watching Seahawks games on TV with Mom and Dad. He likes all the numbers and the cheering and the mascot, a blue bird named Blitz.

"Maybe," I say. I still feel weird about all of the changes this summer. It's like LaTanya and I are on escalators, and hers keeps going up, and mine keeps going down, and we're going to start living on totally different floors. Hers has nice things like a private movie theater and a dachshund named Glitter, and mine has crocodile paint in the bathroom and Grandma Barrel sleeping on the couch in a too-small apartment.

Mom pushes my door open with her foot. She has a mug in one hand and a sponge in the other. "Bathroom," she whispers. "Clean it up. Then I need you to vacuum under the couch cushions. I know Grandma checks."

I give my mom a thumbs-up, but it's a sarcastic thumbs-up.

Beep, beep.

I look at the phone display.

Grandma Barrel is calling.

"Uh, LaTanya, I have to go. My grandma is calling."

"No problem," LaTanya says. "What should I tell my dad? Can you guys come on Sunday?"

Beep, beep.

Aaron would probably really like to see the Seahawks play in real life.

Beep, beep.

And I would probably definitely like to get out of the apartment and away from Grandma Barrel for a day.

Beep, beep.

I'd like to meet LaTanya's dachshund puppy.

And I *know* I can be responsible and babysit Aaron. I've done it at home. Why couldn't I do it at a Seahawks practice? Eagirl would do it. In issue #28, she maneuvers Grizzly Baird's unruly niece cubs out of a wild-horse stampede. I can maneuver one human child through a crowd at a sporting event.

I hold the phone against my chest. "Mom, can Aaron and I go to a Seahawks practice with LaTanya and her dad on Sunday?"

Mom bites her lip. "Yeah. I think so. You deserve some time out after the past couple of weeks. I need you to be really careful, though. Careful with yourself, and careful with Aaron."

I hold the phone back up to my ear. "Yes! My mom says it's okay."

Beep, beep.

"But I really have to go."

"See you on Sunday," LaTanya says.

I press the green "accept" button on the phone.

"Well, I'm glad it only took about an hour for you to answer my phone call," Grandma Barrel says.

"Hi, Grandma Barrel." I hold the phone out to Mom. "It's for you."

She tucks the sponge into the mug she's holding and takes the phone. "Ma! We're excited to see you tomorrow! Yes, just me and the kids tonight. Mm-hmm, he's at his *Lyle, Lyle, Crocodile* rehearsal." She walks back to the kitchen, but I can still hear from my room. "No, I think it's wonderful! No, I'm not upset. I *do* like working at the store. I think it's a great change. Ma, honestly."

Time to clean green paint.

I take the cleaning spray, paper towels, and a trash bag out of the hall closet. Aaron is standing in the doorway of the bathroom.

"C-R-O-C-O-D-I-L-E," he says. "That spells 'crocodile.' M-E-S-S spells 'mess.'"

"You're right, Aaron," I say. There is green paint on the mirror, sink, cabinet, toilet, and shower curtain. It looks like a swamp-monster murder scene. "This is a big, big crocodile mess."

12

Grandma Barrel stands in our doorway wearing a light-blue sun hat and big sunglasses that fit over her regular glasses.

"My goodness," she says, looking around the apartment. "This is quite a step down from your house, isn't it?" She puts her big suitcase down in front of the door and walks in. "And that was such a beautiful house, too. *Tsk.* Such a pity, really."

Dad comes in after her, moving her suitcase to the side. "Actually, it's just fine, Barrel. Change is good." Dad's face is still a little green from rehearsal last night.

"Change isn't always good, my dear," says Grandma Barrel. She sees me on the couch. "Maggie Chowder! Look at you! Come over here and say hello to your grandmother."

I smile a closed-mouth smile and step closer to Grandma Barrel so she can put a hand around my shoulder. Grandma Barrel doesn't really hug. She squeezes me for a couple seconds too long. The rim of her hat pokes the side of my head.

"It's too bad your mother couldn't be here when I arrived. They must be working her to the bone at that grocery store." She makes another *tsk* sound.

"They aren't really working her to the bone," Dad says. "She just started the job. She didn't want to take time off right away."

"And how is your work going, my dear?" Grandma Barrel asks Dad. "Community theater, is it?"

Dad scratches his neck. "No, ah, it's a web series. A modern *Lyle, Lyle, Crocodile*."

"Dad's playing Lyle," I say.

Grandma Barrel removes her sunglasses and squints at him. "Yes, you do look a little green. Well, I can't say I understand any of this, but I'm glad you're having fun."

My cheeks feel hot. I squeeze my hands into fists.

"Dad isn't just 'having fun,'" I say. "He got laid off, and now he brings Aaron to therapy."

"Yes, I know that," says Grandma Barrel. "Anywho. Where is my bedroom?"

I look at Dad.

Dad looks at me.

Aaron looks at Grandma Barrel. "Grandma Barrel is sleeping on the couch," he says. "I want to watch *Diagnosis Murder*." He takes Grandma Barrel by the hand and leads her to the couch.

"'Grandma Barrel is sleeping on the couch,'" grumbles Grandma Barrel. "How wonderful."

Aaron turns on the TV and brings Grandma Barrel the remote.

✖✖✖

I don't like mystery shows. I don't like shows that take place in hospitals, either. Or in offices. They make me feel all closed-in and stuck. Forest rangers work mostly out-doors, or in lookout towers with big windows. I don't think I could ever be a nurse or a doctor. Or somebody working on a computer in an office.

Grandma Barrel and Aaron don't get the same closed-in, stuck feeling. They could watch *Diagnosis Murder* all day long. In our old house, we had two TV rooms. One was the living room, and the other was the den. If Aaron wanted to watch one thing, I could watch something else in the other room. In our apartment, we still have two TVs, but one of them is in Mom and Dad's room because we don't have a den.

Three episodes into *Diagnosis Murder*, I am out of other things to do. My bedroom—our bedroom—is clean, because we don't have that much stuff anymore. Less stuff means it's easier to clean up. I sit down on the couch with Aaron and Grandma Barrel.

"Is this episode almost over?" I ask.

"Shh," says Grandma Barrel. "It's a mystery program. We need to pay attention."

"Shh," says Aaron.

"When this one is over, can we please watch something else?" I ask.

"*Shh*," says Grandma Barrel. "Really, Margaret."

I let out a big, dramatic sigh and get up. Dad is in the kitchen unloading the dishwasher.

"Dad," I say, not loudly enough to get *shh*-ed again. "Can I watch TV in your room? I hate mystery shows and hospital shows. And they're watching a mystery show that's *in* a hospital."

Dad closes the dishwasher door and scratches his chin. "I don't see why not. The remote is probably on your mom's nightstand."

"Thank you!" I practically dance down the hall and into Mom and Dad's room, because Grandma Barrel hasn't even been here a whole day yet and I'm already tired of being around her.

I flop onto Mom and Dad's blue-and-yellow bedspread and reach for the remote on Mom's nightstand. The remote is sitting on top of a small stack of books. I roll over to see which ones she's reading.

The book on top has a picture of two cups of tea on

the cover. It's called *The Art of Being Okay When You're Not Okay*.

Is Mom not okay? She keeps saying that everything's great.

The book underneath the one on top has a picture of a girl dancing under a tree on the cover. *Nature Bathing in the Modern World*. Nature bathing! I flip it over and read the back.

"We are living in a modern world of stress and endless pressure. As a result, our health suffers, our mind suffers, our spirit suffers. *Nature Bathing in the Modern World* is the true story of a woman who ended her own cycle of stress and sickness by spending time in the forest and learning to reconnect with herself."

I don't know whether my spirit is suffering, but I would really, really like to spend some time in a forest. I put the books back exactly the way they were when I came in. I turn the TV on and flip through the available channels to stream. On the Discovery Channel there's a special about red foxes and conservationists. I lean back on Mom's pillow. Hers is softer than mine and smells like her: kind of flowery and a little sweet, like vanilla.

The red fox is one of nature's most cunning animals, and Mike Simpson is determined to keep them from harm. Here, Mike is delivering a lifesaving medication to these two young—

"Margaret!" Grandma Barrel yells from the living room.

I turn down the volume.

"What?" I yell back.

"The picture has gone all...It's hard to see the television. What have you done with it?"

What have I done with *what*? "What are you talking about?" I yell.

"A broken TV," hollers Aaron. "A broken doctor. A broken hospital!"

I hear footsteps in the hallway, and then Dad comes in.

"Ah, sorry, Mags," he says. He really does look sorry. "Now that we cut back on the internet bill, I guess we don't have enough bandwidth to support two TVs going at the same time anymore."

I narrow my eyes. "So why can't Aaron and Grandma Barrel not watch *Diagnosis Murder* for a little while? They've been watching it since she got here!"

Grandma Barrel pushes past Dad into the room. "Because I am your *guest*, Margaret. I would have thought you'd be old enough to understand *respect* and *hospitality* by now." She looks around the room at the empty walls. "You need to hang some nice, homey mementos," she says to Dad. "It's so depressing and bare. Does no one care about making a *home* anymore? It's a simple thing, but it makes *such* a difference." She wrinkles her nose at the blank walls.

Dad rubs the back of his head. "Thanks, Barrel. We'll, uh, get to it."

13

"You don't have any cream cheese?" Grandma Barrel moves around the contents of our refrigerator. "How about Cool Whip? Crushed pineapple? Lime Jell-O? *Nuts*?" She stands up, closes the refrigerator door, and puts her hands on her hips.

"Sorry, Barrel." Dad rubs the back of his neck. "I don't think we have any of that. We moved in pretty recently, and we're still getting settled."

"And anyway, I don't think we've *ever* had most of those things," I say. I don't like how it feels like Grandma Barrel is *accusing* Dad of not keeping us stocked with the weirdest collection of ingredients possible. "Most people don't just have crushed pineapple lying around."

Grandma Barrel sniffs. "*I* do. You never know when you're going to need it."

I turn around before Grandma Barrel can see me roll

my eyes. "Anyway, what are you planning to make?" I sit down at the table.

"Green Jell-O salad. I suppose we'll have to go to your mother's grocery store to pick up what I need." Grandma Barrel shrugs.

Dad and I look at each other. Mom likes *good* surprises, like when Dad brings her breakfast in bed on a random Saturday. She doesn't like bad surprises, and Grandma Barrel is almost always a bad surprise.

"I can run out and pick up what you need, Barrel," says Dad.

"Oh, nooo. I'm very picky about brands, and I like to do my own shopping. I'll go. Maggie can come with me." Grandma Barrel smiles at me.

I try to smile back, but I really don't feel like it.

Grandma Barrel drums her opaly painted nails on the side of the fridge. "What else should I pick up while we're out? The refrigerator is just so empty," she says, mostly to herself.

Aaron perks up from his seat on the couch. "Aaahh!" he says. "There's a dirty diaper under the fridge!" He laughs like he's just said the funniest thing on earth.

"There's a...*Pardon me*?" Grandma Barrel drops her hand and looks at Aaron in horror.

I bite my lip to keep from laughing. "I'll get my shoes on," I say.

The walk to Mom's grocery store is cool and breezy, and the sidewalk is littered with slugs the way it always is after it rains in Renton. I dodge them easily, like most kids who have lived here since birth.

Grandma Barrel wrinkles her nose. "What is all of this? Dog droppings?"

"Slugs," I say.

Grandma Barrel unwrinkles her nose. "Really?" She bends over to look at a slug more closely. "Fascinating. They are enormous."

I think slugs are fascinating, but I didn't expect Grandma Barrel to think so, too.

"These giant black slugs—are they native to Washington?"

I shake my head. "Invasive."

Grandma Barrel straightens up, and we keep walking. Blackberry vines loop around trees and weave in and out of stone walls. "These are invasive too," I say, carefully moving an aggressive-looking thorny vine out of our way with my fingertips.

"Yes, Himalayan blackberries. I watched a Discovery Channel special all about them."

I look at Grandma Barrel in surprise. "You watch the Discovery Channel? That's my favorite channel." We walk in silence for a minute. If Grandma Barrel watches interesting nature shows, why do we always have to watch *Diagnosis Murder* when she's visiting?

"Aaron enjoys *Diagnosis Murder*," Grandma Barrel says, as if reading my mind.

✖✖✖

When we reach the grocery store, I have a fluttery feeling in my stomach. It's going to be *weird* to see Mom at work. Especially when I have Grandma Barrel with me. Especially when Mom has no idea we're here.

"Let's see," says Grandma Barrel, pulling her shopping list out of her purse. "Chopped nuts. Those will be in the baking aisle." I pick up a basket and follow Grandma Barrel to aisle eleven. I'm watching everyone around me, looking for Mom's familiar braid and freckles.

"Oh. My. Wow." says a voice that is familiar, but not nearly as familiar as Mom's. I turn around, and my eyeballs are assaulted by Jenna Kapow and her spiky-on-one-side hair, neon-pink eye shadow, and lemon-yellow suit. This time, her single earring is a dangling planet Saturn.

"Do you know this woman?" Grandma Barrel whispers in my ear.

"Megan! Meggie Meg, it is a *blast* to see you again.

107

Aah!" She pulls me into a hug I am not prepared for. When she lets me go, she sees Grandma Barrel. "Oh, hello!" Jenna Kapow jabs out one hand for Grandma Barrel to shake. "Jenna Kapow, Not-Quite-Seattle Realty."

"I'm *Megan's* grandmother, Barrel," says Grandma Barrel, looking at me slyly out of the corner of her eye. She pumps Jenna Kapow's hand one time, then lets go. "And how do you know my granddaughter?"

"I sold her beautiful house!" Jenna Kapow says brightly.

I feel Grandma Barrel darken next to me. "I see."

"It was an easy sale, too. Such a great home. And how are you loving your *new* home, Megan?"

I swallow. "It's really great," I say.

"We should get back to our shopping," says Grandma Barrel.

"Oh, is Granny making something special for you and your sweet widdle brother?" Jenna Kapow twirls her dangly Saturn earring.

I cringe.

"I'm planning to make a green Jell-O salad," says Grandma Barrel.

Jenna Kapow's mouth drops open. "A green Jell-O *salad*?" For the first time, I notice the contents of her shopping cart. Mostly leafy-green vegetables. Something called Peanut Butter Protein Powder. Agave nectar. "My granny used to make that. There's nothing *salad* about it! I ate it when I was a kid. I didn't know better back then." She laughs. "It's all hydrogenated vegetable oil and Yellow 5 food dye." She makes a grossed-out face.

Grandma Barrel stares at Jenna Kapow with such intensity that I want to hide behind the display of disposable baking pans. "And which number of yellow is that *tremendously* offensive suit you're wearing, I wonder?"

Jenna Kapow frowns. "Well, it was nice to see you, Megan."

"You too," I say, looking at my shoes.

Jenna Kapow backs her cart away from us.

"Ahh," says Grandma Barrel, pulling a red bag off the shelf. "Chopped nuts."

I can't decide whether Grandma Barrel is just plain rude, or if she's like a superhero. *Fending off rudeness with rudeness, awkwardly ending bad conversations in a flash.*

"The lime Jell-O is in the next aisle," I say. We turn the corner. "It's right over here—"

But the lime Jell-O isn't all that's right over here.

Mom is standing next to the Jell-O, looking exhausted and wary. Her braid is all pulled out and messy, and there is flour on her pant legs. She is eyeing me with a little annoyance. "You should have let me know you were coming."

"I'm not allowed to have a cell phone," I say. "If I did, I would have texted you."

Now she is eyeing me with a *lot* of annoyance.

Then she looks at Grandma Barrel.

"Hi, Ma," she says.

14

"Well, just look at you," Grandma Barrel says to Mom.

"Yep, look at me. Working at my job. Which I have to get back to in a minute." Mom brushes off her pants, but it doesn't make a difference. They still have flour all over them. She sighs, and I remember the book in her room. *The Art of Being Okay When You're Not Okay.*

"We're here to get stuff for Grandma Barrel's green Jell-O salad," I say helpfully.

"I used to love that when I was a kid." Mom picks a small fruit sticker off the side of her shoe. "I'll see you both back at home, okay?" She reaches out and squeezes my hand. "Good to see you, Ma. We'll catch up tonight." She nods at Grandma Barrel.

Grandma Barrel and I collect the rest of the ingredients and then check out. On our way out of the store, Grandma Barrel stops me at the big bulletin board of community notices and advertisements.

"Is this your friend?" She points to an in-color ad with a picture of Jenna Kapow high-kicking the side of a house. It says:

Jenna Kapow, Not-Quite-Seattle Realty
Selling your house before you can say KAPOW!

"Terrible," says Grandma Barrel.

Underneath Jenna Kapow's ad, there is a poster for Seattle Comic Con.

SEATTLE COMIC CON
July 14–17
Washington State Convention Center
"Let your inner superhero out!"

The picture shows people dressed up as all kinds of superheroes and cartoon characters. Somebody is dressed up as a crocodile. His snout is more professional-looking than Dad's. In tiny letters all across the middle of the ad there is a list of the comic-book creators who will be there.

"Nora Cho!" I gasp. "She makes the Eagirl comics!"

Next to Nora Cho's name, there is an asterisk.

At the bottom of the page, there is a second asterisk next to the best news I have heard in months.

Nora Cho will host an Eagirl costume contest. Enter and wear your best Eagirl costume on July 14 for a chance to win one FULL scholarship to Junior Forest Ranger Camp.

"Mmm. You certainly do like your comic books," Grandma Barrel says. She sounds like she still thinks I'm too old to read comics, but I'm too excited to care.

"I *have* to go to this, Grandma Barrel," I say. "I have to meet Nora Cho."

"And do what?" asks Grandma Barrel.

"And…and tell her that I love her comics. And that Eagirl is the reason I want to be a forest ranger. And enter this costume contest so I can win a full scholarship to Junior Forest Ranger Camp!"

"You still want to be a forest ranger? I didn't realize. You don't call me very often, so I never know *what* you're interested in."

"I've always wanted to be a forest ranger. When I was little, and now."

"Well, I wish your mother would have mentioned it to me. I wish *you* would have mentioned it to me."

I ignore Grandma Barrel's obvious annoyance. I am too excited about the Junior Forest Ranger Camp opportunity to let even Grandma Barrel bring me down.

"Well, I still do," I say. "Ever since I started reading Eagirl comics. I already know which forestry college I want to go to after I graduate from high school. And I've always, always wanted to go to Junior Forest Ranger Camp, but it's way too expensive."

"Mmm," Grandma Barrel says again. "I didn't realize there *was* a Junior Forest Ranger Camp."

"There is! It's right at the bottom of Mount Rainier. You get to live in a cabin for two weeks and take courses on forest safety, and you go on all kinds of hikes and study native plants and animals and learn first aid, but it costs a lot. But Comic Con *doesn't* cost that much, and I could—"

"You could win," says Grandma Barrel. She squints at the poster. "Fine." She looks at the ceiling and mouths a couple of numbers, as though trying to figure out which day July 14 falls on. "This Seattle Comic Con is just over a week away. Your father will have to bring Aaron to therapy that day, and your mother will be working. I suppose I could take you."

"Really?" My mouth is hanging open. Seattle Comic Con is the *last* place I would expect Grandma Barrel to want to go.

"Yes. You know I don't like comics, Margaret, and I think you're quite old enough to read books without pictures. But if you did win this…costume contest, you would have the opportunity to go to your Junior Forest Ranger Camp. *That* is a worthwhile way to spend your time."

"Thank you, Grandma Barrel." For the first time since the tree fell on our car, I feel like this summer might be okay after all. "Now I just need to figure out a costume."

***

That night, Grandma Barrel is at the kitchen table working on a puzzle with Aaron. Mom is tucking the pink-striped guest sheets into the couch cushions, and I am tugging white pillow cases with little yellow flowers on them onto the extra pillows.

"I'm sorry about just showing up today," I say.

Mom shrugs. "You don't have to be sorry. I can hardly expect people not to go to the store. You just caught me by surprise."

"Do you like working at the grocery store?" I ask. I think about the flour on her pants and the fruit sticker she picked off of her shoe.

Mom lays a fleece blanket over the couch. "You know what? It's not so bad."

"Did you know," Grandma Barrel says loudly, so

116

Mom can hear her from the table, "that your daughter still wants to be a forest ranger?"

"I *did* know that, actually," says Mom. She smiles at me.

"I'm relieved, frankly, that *some*one in this family has career aspirations."

Mom makes her mouth into a tight line. She takes the pillow from me and tosses it onto the end of the couch.

"Margaret, did you know that your mother went to cooking school? She did. A good one, too. Two years. She was going to be a cook."

"It was a pastry school," Mom says quietly.

"Ah, yes. Pastry school. To be a pastry chef. Wouldn't that have been something?" Grandma Barrel sighs. "To have a pastry chef in the family. Oh, well."

The front door closes.

Dad steps in with his *Lyle* script in one hand. His face looks serious. He almost never looks serious. He joins me and Mom at the couch and wraps Mom up in a hug.

"She *is* something, Barrel," Dad says. "She's amazing." He kisses Mom on top of her head.

"I'm going to get Aaron ready for bed, and then I'm going to go to bed myself. I'm pretty tired," says Mom.

"I'll do the same," says Dad. "Rehearsal was great, but it was long."

I realize then that we all have to go to bed. Because

Grandma Barrel is going to be sleeping in our living room, and our living room is attached to the dining room. There's nowhere else to *be* in this apartment other than our bedrooms.

"Good night, I guess," I say.

"No," says Aaron, who is still working on his puzzle with Grandma Barrel. "I am not all done."

"Sorry, buddy," says Mom. "It's past your bedtime."

"I am *not* all *done*! I am not all done," cries Aaron, frantically trying to fit the puzzle piece he is holding into empty spots in the puzzle.

Mom sighs. "Buddy."

"I am not all *done*," says Aaron, with a big fat tear rolling down his face.

I am, I think. *Done with this day. Done with Grandma Barrel's visit. Done with this summer.*

I go to my room, close the door, and change into my pajamas before Aaron and Mom come in.

In the morning, Dad takes Aaron to therapy. I try to avoid Grandma Barrel, but the apartment is so small that I can't. When I want to get a glass of water, Grandma Barrel is rinsing out a cup in the kitchen sink.

"What is 'occupational therapy'?" she asks. "I asked your father, but you know one cannot get a straight answer from him about anything."

I glare at her. "It's like...It's just a therapy Aaron needs."

"Ahh, enlightening," Grandma Barrel says sarcastically. "Thank you *so* much for your help."

Coping mechanisms, I remember. It gives Aaron coping mechanisms. It helps him deal with sensory issues. But I don't feel like explaining it to Grandma Barrel now. If she wants to know so badly, she can go spend some time with Eva in the waiting room.

When I want to read *The Exceptional Eagirl #44* on the

balcony, Grandma Barrel is already out there, drinking a cup of tea and reading the newspaper. She raises her eyebrow at my comic book when I sit down next to her.

"Your mother is bringing home materials I've requested to make your costume. I've found a pattern that should be satisfactory. You and I will work on it together tonight." She sighs. "And you know, Margaret, there is literature that will be more helpful to you and your forest ranger aspirations than *comics*. Actual books, for instance. Books on law enforcement. Books on forestry. I believe I *gave* you these books once for your birthday."

The birthday of the suitcase and the old books. I guess I hadn't paid attention to what *kind* of old books they were.

"Thanks for helping with my costume, Grandma Barrel." I smile at her, but I'm also wondering what the costume will look like. Whether Grandma Barrel actually expects me to sew. I've never sewn anything in my entire life. Can something we make in a night actually win the contest? Probably not. I have a really bad feeling that it's going to be a droopy old sack with some feathers stuck to it.

I take my comic book back inside and read on my bed next to Anderson Cooper.

Grandma Barrel is everywhere. The kitchen, the living room, the balcony. She's like a cranky ghost haunting my apartment. I'm relieved when I hear Dad unlock the door.

"We're home!" he calls.

"Good," I mutter.

✖✖✖

Lunch is a plate full of *things,* which is what we always have in the summer. Today the *things* are carrot sticks, hummus, Goldfish crackers, sliced cheese, and strawberries.

"My favorites," Aaron says. He says this whenever we have a plate of *things.* He never says it when we have an actual big meal. I don't understand why we don't just have a plate of *things* for every meal, but Mom got annoyed when I suggested that during dinner one night, so I haven't brought it up since.

"My favorites, too, Aaron," I say. I pop a strawberry into my mouth.

"I'm sorry, is this *lunch?*" says Grandma Barrel. She holds a Goldfish cracker up and examines it.

"Yes," I say.

Dad is in the kitchen pouring a cup of milk for Aaron. He clenches his jaw and looks up at the ceiling.

"And what is this?" Grandma Barrel waves her hand over the hummus.

"That's hummus. It's good," I say.

Grandma Barrel wrinkles her nose. "I'll pass. In my day, lunch was something real, like a sandwich."

122

Dad closes his eyes.

I make my hands into fists again under the table. I can practically see the shadow of Hawkmare on the wall behind Grandma Barrel. If I were Eagirl, I would jump out of my chair and point my finger in her face. I would say, "If you want to keep all of your feathers, I suggest you leave now."

But I'm not Eagirl. And Grandma Barrel isn't just my nemesis. She's also my mom's mother. And Mom would be really, really mad if I made Grandma Barrel leave. And besides, I'm pretty sure the only way I'm going to get to go to Comic Con and meet Nora Cho and enter that costume contest is if Grandma Barrel takes me.

Grandma Barrel leans over the container of hummus and sniffs it. She wrinkles her face up like she smells something bad.

I see red. I can't help it. I don't care if she *is* my ticket to meeting Nora Cho.

"If you aren't going to eat it, don't put your nose in it," I say. I slide the hummus away from Grandma Barrel. She sits back with her mouth open.

"I have *never* heard anything so rude in my—"

"You think *I'm* the rude one?" I stand up fast, knocking my chair over. "All you do is complain! You complain about the couch. You complain about not having ugly, boring things on the walls. You complain about Dad. You complain

123

about Mom's job. You complain about what we eat and where we live. If you're just going to complain about everything, why did you come here in the first—"

Grandma Barrel's eyes are very wide. And right behind her is my mom, who is very quiet when she enters an apartment, I guess. Mom's eyes aren't wide. She doesn't even look that angry. But I know better. When she looks perfectly calm, that's when she's angriest.

Her voice is quiet and low. "Margaret Michelle Chowder. You need to go to your room *immediately*. Immediately."

I want to tell her that's not fair. I want to tell her how Grandma Barrel has been rude and nasty ever since she got here, and how this is how she *always* is—how this is why I didn't want her to come at all—but I don't tell her that. Her face is calm and her eyes are glittering like ice. She seems a foot taller than usual. I pick my chair up and push it back to the table. I go to my room and close the door.

I put my ear against the inside of the door. I can hear Mom apologizing to Grandma Barrel. I hear Grandma Barrel saying things like *Well, I never* and *You have to teach that girl to respect her elders*. A quiet *tap-tap* on the other side of my door makes me jump. I open it, and Dad is standing there.

"Can I come in?"

"Yeah," I say.

I flop onto Aaron's bunk. Dad sits down next to me.

"So, obviously, don't, you know. Don't say those things to your grandmother." Dad ruffles his hair with his hand. "Especially if your mom is around."

"She *wasn't* around," I say. "She just appeared out of nowhere!"

"Yeah, she'll do that. So maybe it's just safer not to say those things to your grandmother at all."

I narrow my eyes at Dad. "But she was being *so* awful. Did you see how she was sniffing the hummus? '*I'm sorry, is this lunch?*' I mean, Dad! She said our apartment is a big step down from the house. She said she's glad you're just *having fun* while they work Mom to the bone at the grocery store. She's so *mean*."

Dad nods and looks up at the ceiling. "But, kiddo, aren't those some of the same feelings you've been having, too?"

I don't know why, but my eyes prickle with tears. I don't want Dad to see. I stare at a spot on the wall and focus on drying my eyes out.

"Haven't you been having a really hard time with all these changes? I mean, you seem like you're dealing with it all pretty well. But hasn't it been hard for you?" Dad is looking at me. I can tell. I keep staring at the wall, willing the tears to go away. One of them spills out of my eye and rolls down my cheek, and then I know it's all over. I'm going to cry. I *hate* crying. Especially in front of people. Especially when I'm trying to seem brave and like I can handle this stuff. Eagirl almost never cries.

"It wouldn't…be so bad"—I sniff—"if it was just like one thing at a time." I take a deep, shuddery breath. "It's *everything*. All at once. I used to tell LaTanya everything. We told each other everything. But now her life is getting so good, and my life is getting so bad. I don't want to hear about her stuff, and I don't want her to know about mine." The tears keep coming, hot and fast.

I'm only kind of aware of my mom standing in the doorway.

"Why?" Dad says. "Why don't you want her to know about your stuff?"

I shrug. "I guess because I'm embarrassed."

"Of what?" Mom asks quietly.

I shrug again.

"LaTanya is your best friend. Whether you're in an apartment or a mansion, whether your dad is a crocodile or an oil tycoon, she's your best friend. And you don't have to be embarrassed."

Mom sits down on the other side of me. She and Dad squeeze me into a big, tight hug. Tears keep falling onto my T-shirt for a while, but eventually they stop. And then we all sit up. I feel better. Like I don't have to carry around such a heavy sack anymore. I don't know how to make the embarrassed feeling go away, but saying it out loud made the feeling a little smaller.

"I love you both," I say.

"We love you too, honey," says Mom. "We're here to listen to you when you're having a hard time. That's kind of our job."

"Thanks," I say. I wipe my nose with my arm.

"Do you know who else loves you?" Mom is smiling kind of apologetically, and I know what's coming next.

"Ugh. Probably Grandma Barrel."

"Definitely Grandma Barrel," says Mom.

"Sooo…she might feel better if you go out there and say you're sorry," says Dad. He spreads his hands out like *Sorry, but what can I say?*

Ugh.

"In the future, you can totally tell her how you feel without, you know, yelling at her and throwing chairs around," says Dad.

"I didn't *throw* the chair," I say. I try not to smile but can't help it. The image of me throwing a chair at the wall like Grizzly Baird is kind of funny.

"Even so," says Mom.

At the kitchen table, Aaron is showing off his spelling skills to Grandma Barrel.

"C-R-O-C-O-D-I-L-E," he says. "That spells 'crocodile.'"

"*Crocodile,*" says Grandma Barrel. She turns to look at us.

"Did you all hear that? This child can spell 'crocodile'! Four-year-olds don't know how to spell 'crocodile '."

"This one does," says Dad.

"W-O-R-K," says Aaron. "M-I-C-E."

"Are you hearing this?" says Grandma Barrel.

"Yes," Mom and Dad say at the same time.

"G-O-O-P. I like goop," says Aaron.

"This child is a genius!" says Grandma Barrel. "Aaron, my dear, you are an absolute genius."

"Grandma," I say, "I'm sorry I yelled at you."

Grandma Barrel flutters her hand in my direction, but she is still looking at Aaron. "That's fine, dear. It's fine."

✖✖✖

That night, Grandma Barrel and I spread brown faux-leather fabric, feathers, needles, thread, buttons, and linen all over the table. There's gray fabric there, too.

"What's that for?" I ask.

"Your sidekick," says Grandma Barrel. She sits up a little straighter in her chair. "Possum Sauce."

My mouth drops open. "My *sidekick*? How do you even know about Possum Sauce?"

"I do know how to read, Margaret," Grandma Barrel says. "I believe it will give you a competitive edge to have a sidekick, dear. I will wear a Possum Sauce costume. And *you* will make it for me. Do you know how to use a sewing machine?"

"No, I definitely do not."

Grandma Barrel smiles. "Wonderful! We'll start at the beginning." She points to something sticking out of the top of the sewing machine. "This is called a 'spool pin.'"

✖✖✖

We work until eleven thirty, cutting fabric, lining it up under the needle, pressing lightly on the foot pedal. We sew the feathers and buttons on by hand.

We aren't finished yet, but the Eagirl costume already looks really good. The stitches are all straight, and it doesn't bunch up at any of the seams, like Grandma Barrel's Possum Sauce costume does.

"Sorry about your costume," I say to Grandma Barrel.

"Oh, I think it's a fine job for a first sewing project," says Grandma Barrel.

I think it's probably also my *last* sewing project, but I don't tell her that.

My Eagirl costume is probably not going to win the contest, but it's not nearly as bad as a droopy old sack.

We hang our costumes from the balcony-door curtain rod.

"We'll finish tomorrow," Grandma Barrel says, looking thoughtfully at the costumes. "A fine job," she says again.

16

It's so early in the morning that it's still dark outside my bedroom window. *Our* bedroom window. I hear Aaron softly snoring in his bunk. Was it Aaron's snoring that woke me up? I don't think so. I feel around for Anderson Cooper, but he isn't there. Aaron must have him again.

Clink.

Someone is in the kitchen.

Clink, clink. Then the loud *errrrr* of the coffee maker.

Maybe there are two someones in the kitchen. I hear quiet, murmury voices.

"When I was a young lady," says one of the people in the kitchen, "I had a newspaper route. I wasn't reading comic books."

Grandma Barrel. I rub my eyes and sit up. I doubt they even *had* comic books when Grandma Barrel was a young lady.

"Ma, please," says the other person in the kitchen. My mother. "I love that Maggie reads. It doesn't really matter *what* she reads."

"Oh, we do have different styles of parenting, don't we?" says Grandma Barrel.

Good, I think. Because Grandma Barrel's style of parenting stinks.

"She wants to be a forest ranger," says Mom. "And her comics are kind of feminist forest-ranger literature." I get a warm feeling in my chest.

"Do you know what would prepare her for becoming a forest ranger? That camp she wants to attend. What is it called? Junior Forest Ranger Camp. Something like that," says Grandma Barrel.

I bite my lip.

"Well, that camp is awfully expensive." Mom sounds upset. "I would give my kids the whole world if I could, and I think you know that, Ma. But we can't afford camp right now."

I climb down the ladder and drop to the floor.

"Stay in your bed," Aaron says. I jump, startled. He is sitting straight up in his bunk, looking at me. Anderson Cooper is in his lap. "Stay in your bed until seven o'clock."

He's right. That's the rule. But it's only the rule because our parents don't want Aaron waking them up before seven.

If they're already awake, the rule doesn't count.

"Another rule is *Don't take Anderson Cooper without asking me*," I say.

Aaron narrows his eyes at me. He lies back down with his head on his pillow, clutching Anderson Cooper's soft body to his chin.

I open the door and close it again quietly, sneaking down the hallway. At the end of the hallway, I can see the dining room table. Mom and Grandma are sitting there, drinking their coffee in silence.

"Good morning," I say.

"Good morning," says Grandma Barrel.

"Morning," says Mom, glancing at the time on the oven clock. "Why are you up so early?"

"I heard the coffee maker," I say. I pull out a chair and sit down next to Mom.

"Oh, yes," says Mom. She looks at Grandma Barrel. "Maggie drinks coffee with us now."

I get a bitter taste in my mouth just remembering the black coffee from the other morning.

"Would you like a cup, honey?" asks Mom.

I would not, and I almost tell her that, but Grandma Barrel jumps in first.

"Coffee is *not* a beverage for a twelve-year-old girl," she says to Mom. "Honestly, I don't know where your head is,

Heidi. You let her read comic books like a five-year-old and drink coffee like a twenty-year-old."

"Five-year-olds don't read," I say. "And I would *love* a cup of coffee."

"Your brother is only four, and he certainly *does* read," says Grandma Barrel.

"Both of you, *please*," says Mom. She rests her forehead on her fingertips. "I need your help. I need you to get along and to *help* me. I don't need you to make things harder."

I feel bad. I feel *mad*, because sometimes Grandma Barrel is the worst, but I feel bad for my mom.

Mom gets up and makes me a cup of coffee. She uses the blue PNW mug with the tree on the bottom. When she sets it in front of me, I shudder. It smells so good, and I know it's going to taste so bad.

Mom looks at me curiously. I wonder if she saw my shudder. I'm not very good at hiding the shuddering. "Do you want some milk in it, honey?" she asks.

"Sure," I say. That isn't how Eagirl or forest rangers drink *their* coffee, but I tried it their way and it wasn't good.

She adds a splash of milk to my coffee, and I watch it swirl and blossom out until the coffee is the color of caramel. I take a sip. It isn't exactly *good*, but it is better. I take another sip and lock eyes with Grandma Barrel over the rim of my mug.

"As you know, Margaret and I are going to attend the Seattle Comic Con. That's what those costumes we're making are for." She takes a sip of her coffee and glances toward the curtain rod.

"Margaret wants to meet the creator of her comic books. Now, I am uninterested in comics, as you know. I don't think they are appropriate for a girl her age. But she did express that her comics have kindled her desire to be a forest ranger, and I can certainly appreciate that."

"Well, great," says Mom. She looks at me with one raised eyebrow.

"Now, I suspect Junior Forest Ranger Camp would be far more beneficial to Margaret, but it seems that isn't in the cards for her this summer," says Grandma Barrel.

"It's about two months of rent," says Mom. "That's how expensive it is to go to Junior Forest Ranger Camp." She makes a sad, tight-lipped smile at me. "Someday you'll go, I promise. But money stuff is a little hard right now."

"Well," says Grandma Barrel. "I like a person who is serious about things. I like a person who doesn't mess around with foolish things and who really dedicates herself to a serious discipline like law enforcement in forestry. It's a shame that Margaret cannot afford to go to Junior Forest Ranger Camp at the moment. However, at this Comic Con, the creator of her comic books is hosting a costume contest.

The winner of the contest will be awarded a full scholarship to Junior Forest Ranger Camp. I believe Margaret can win the contest. Her costume is sufficient, and so is mine."

My costume is still missing all of the feathers down one faux leather arm, and Grandma Barrel's really needs a pink possum tail. Our costumes are good, but they aren't professional or expensive. I picture Grandma Barrel and I lined up with all of the other Eagirls in professional, expensive Eagirl costumes. I bite my lip. I don't want Grandma Barrel to feel too bad when she realizes we're definitely, *definitely* not going to win.

But it was really cool of her to stay up all night and work on the costumes with me. Grandma Barrel is the only person I know who can be so horrible and so *not* horrible in the same week.

"I think that's a great idea and a fun thing for you two to do together," says Mom.

"As I said, I despise foolishness and appreciate a person who dedicates herself to a serious discipline."

I hear footsteps in the hallway, and then Dad enters the dining room wearing his pajamas, with his crocodile snout strapped to his face. Aaron follows him, giggling softly.

"Good morning, everybody!" Dad winks at us.

Grandma Barrel closes her eyes and takes another sip of her coffee.

LaTanya calls on Dad's phone after lunch. He holds it out to me, and I take the phone out to the balcony. I can *almost* imagine I live somewhere really nice when I'm out on the balcony. Out in the breeze that just happens to smell a little like the dumpster on the other side of the building. Surrounded by flowers, even if they are invasive.

"Hey!" I say into the phone.

"Maggie! I am *dying* to hang out. Seriously. Can I come over? I am so bored. Boooorrreddd. You can't even imagine. I have *nothing* to do. I haven't seen another human being all day. My mom has a commercial shoot in the fountain garden out back, and my dad is at training camp. I need to see an actual face!"

LaTanya's new house has a fountain garden? I look inside through the sliding door. Aaron is messily eating a bowl of Grandma Barrel's leftover green Jell-O salad. Grandma Barrel is gesturing frantically to a stripe of green face paint on the wall in the living room. Dad's snout is on, and he is all green. He must have rubbed against the wall by accident. He runs into the bathroom, probably to get a wet cloth to wipe down the wall. Or maybe just to fix his makeup. It's hard to know.

Everything in my apartment is green.

"Um, how about I come over to your house instead?"

"Yes! That would be great! I don't care where we hang out. I just miss you," says LaTanya.

I open the sliding door and cover the mouthpiece of the phone.

"Dad, can I go to LaTanya's today?"

Dad stops wiping the second streak of green face paint Grandma Barrel found on the light switch. "Um…Yeah, I don't see why not. Are her parents home?"

"Her mom is, but she's shooting a commercial in her backyard."

"A commercial?" says Dad. "Wow! Man. What a life. Sure, I'll bring you over on my way."

HAVE YOU HEARD THE STORIES ABOUT EAGIRL?

WHO?

LEGEND HAS IT, SHE WAS JUST A BABY WHEN HER HUMAN MOTHER ABANDONED HER.

AN EAGLE FOUND HER CRYING ON THE FOREST FLOOR. SHE TOOK THE BABY HOME, TREATED HER LIKE SHE WAS HER OWN BABY, AND RAISED EAGIRL.

THAT'S A SAD STORY.

IT GETS WORSE. EAGIRL'S BIOLOGICAL MOTHER TURNED OUT TO BE A TERRIBLE VILLAIN—EAGIRL'S OWN NEMESIS—FOREST FIERA.

FOREST FIERA IS THE WORST CRIMINAL THE FORESTS OF THE PACIFIC NORTHWEST HAVE EVER SEEN. AS LONG AS SHE STILL HAUNTS THESE FORESTS, SO DOES EAGIRL.

17

LaTanya's new house is only an eight-minute car ride away from my apartment, but it looks like it's in a completely different town. Where my apartment is all rough and beige and gray on the outside, LaTanya's giant house is pink and green with white stones all around it. There are bushes shaped like animals—dolphins, tigers, flamingos—in gold pots all along her wide, white driveway.

"Wow," I say.

"Wow is right." Dad whistles. "This is some house!"

We pull up in front of the house, and LaTanya rushes out to meet us.

"You're here!"

I unbuckle and jump out of the car. "I'm here! And your house—holy cow!"

Dad lowers his window and sticks his crocodile snout

out. "Hey there, LaTanya! What kind of commercial is your mom shooting?"

"It's for some kind of local landscaping company," says LaTanya. "They did the fountains, I guess?"

Dad shakes his head. "That is just about the coolest thing I have ever heard. Well, you two have fun! Maggie, I'll pick you up in a couple of hours when we're done shooting my bathtub scene!"

Dad pulls out of the driveway, and I follow LaTanya up her big, smooth front steps.

"Sorry about my dad," I say, "He's pretty weird these days, and he's always around."

"Your dad cracks me up," LaTanya says. "I've barely even seen my dad this week."

LaTanya opens the green double doors to the house, and I gasp. She really does live in a mansion. The first room I see is enormous, and there isn't even anything in it besides a little glass table with a vase of flowers on it.

"Should I...take my shoes off?" I ask her. I never took my shoes off when I went inside LaTanya's old house, but this new house is about a million times fancier.

LaTanya gives me a strange look. "No! Why would you?"

A tiny brown dog scrabbles into the room and runs excited circles around our ankles.

"This is Glitter," says LaTanya. She picks up the puppy and kisses it on its head.

"He's so cute!" I say. I rub Glitter behind his ear. It's the softest thing I've ever felt.

He stretches his tiny neck out to try to lick my hand, but he can't quite reach.

"Let's grab a snack, and I'll show you my room."

LaTanya leads me into the kitchen, carrying Glitter in the crook of her elbow like a baby. The kitchen is bright white. All of the cabinets are white, the floors are white, and the island in the middle is white with sparkling gold specks all over the top. LaTanya presses a button on the refrigerator, and suddenly a picture of the inside of the fridge appears on a screen on one of the refrigerator doors.

"Whoa," I say.

"It's so you can see what's in there without standing in front of the fridge with the door open. It saves energy," says LaTanya.

We decide on apple slices and cheesecake fruit dip. I cut up the apples, and LaTanya scoops the dip into a bowl.

"Let's take it up to my room," she says.

I feel weird taking food anywhere but the kitchen in this house. Everything is so *clean*. And expensive-looking.

I feel a little better when LaTanya opens the door to her bedroom. It's big and just as expensive-looking as the other rooms I've seen, but all of LaTanya's old stuff is there, too. She closes her door so Glitter can't get in.

"He'll bug us for apples. I'll let him in after we're done."

Her bed is messy, and the little brown Seattle bear I bought her before she went on vacation in Vancouver is half-tucked in on top of her pillow. Her framed gumwrapper autograph is on top of her dresser. LaTanya's walls are covered in her Dahlia, Queen Warrior posters. I didn't realize I was worried that her gum wrapper and posters would be gone until I saw them there. My eyes get kind of hot and watery, and I blink a few times and sit down cross-legged on the floor with the plate of apple slices. Same LaTanya. Different house.

LaTanya sits down across from me and puts down the bowl of dip.

"Your house is really amazing," I say.

"Yeah, I guess," says LaTanya. "But it's also too big and too quiet."

I think about the messy, green scene in my apartment right before I came over.

"You're lucky," I say. "Mine is too small and too loud."

LaTanya doesn't say anything. I bite into a piece of apple and look at her posters again. Dahlia, Queen Warrior is in the same comic universe as Eagirl. I swallow.

"Oh! Grandma Barrel is taking me to Comic Con. Do you

want to go, too? Nora Cho, the creator of Eagirl, will be there."

LaTanya's eyes light up. "I'm supposed to go with my mom and dad, because the Seahawks are doing a meet and greet at Comic Con. But I bet we can meet up! Oh man, I hope there is some Dahlia, Queen Warrior stuff there. I just finished her new comic, and it was probably the best one yet."

"I'm an entire issue behind on *Exceptional Eagirl*," I say. The comic book store is too far to walk from our apartment, and our one car is always in use.

"I can't wait to see all the costumes," says LaTanya, still thinking about Comic Con.

"Yeah!" I say. "Actually, there's going to be a contest—"

There is a burst of loud cheering outside LaTanya's bedroom window. We both get up and look out at the fountain garden to see what's going on. LaTanya's mom and a bunch of other people are looking at something on a video monitor.

"They must have wrapped," says LaTanya.

There are lights on giant poles, even though it's light outside. There are roses floating around in one of the fountains, like somebody just threw them in there. LaTanya's mom looks more like Dahlia than she ever has before—she is wearing a bunch of drapey gold necklaces and a flowy, white sleeveless dress.

"Your mom is beautiful," I say.

"Yeah," says LaTanya. She sighs. "I hope she doesn't invite everybody in."

LaTanya was just talking about how her house is too quiet. I wonder why she doesn't want her mom's commercial people to come in.

We hear a door close downstairs, and Glitter begins whining more urgently on the other side of LaTanya's bedroom door. LaTanya moves the apples and dip to her desk. She opens her door to let the puppy inside, and Glitter runs in, wagging his tiny tail appreciatively. LaTanya scoops him up and puts him on top of her bed. He runs in a couple of fast circles, resembling a doughnut for a few seconds, and lies down with a contented sigh.

"The commercial crew was here yesterday to do a lighting and sound check, and when they came in for coffee and snacks, one of them stepped on Glitter. They didn't even see him because he's so small." LaTanya looks sadly at Glitter.

"Oh no! Poor puppy," I say.

"They barely know I'm here, either," says LaTanya.

I don't know what to say to her, so I pick up another apple slice and take a bite. Glitter perks one ear up at the *crunch* sound.

"Is Glitter coming with us to the Seahawks practice on Sunday?" I ask.

LaTanya shakes her head. "I asked. Mom said no,

because he might get squished. I told her he *already* got squished, and right here in our own house."

"What did she say after that?"

"She said, 'LaTanya, your attitude has got to *change*.'"

I nod. "I've been getting that a *lot* lately."

We finish our snack and play a few rounds of Uno on LaTanya's floor. Almost exactly like old times, except everything is bigger and fancier.

When my dad rings the doorbell, we go downstairs.

"Sorry, Glitter," says LaTanya, closing her door with the puppy inside. "The crew's still here. It's not safe for you downstairs."

We open the double doors in the front of the house.

"Wow," Dad says. He sees the enormous, almost-empty front room with its high ceiling before he sees me. "Oh, hey, Mags. You about ready to go home?"

"Yep," I say. But he isn't looking at me. He's looking past me into the kitchen, where the commercial crew is eating and laughing with LaTanya's mom.

Dad waves into the kitchen, but no one waves back. I don't think anyone in there even sees us.

"See you on Sunday," I say to LaTanya.

"Yeah." She sighs. "See you then." She glances sadly in the direction of the kitchen. "I'll be hanging out in my room with Glitter if you want to talk on the phone later."

"Okay, maybe!" I say.

LaTanya closes the door behind us.

xxx

In the car on the way home, Dad is quiet. I wonder if he's thinking about LaTanya's enormous house. When he pulls into our parking spot at the apartment, he pauses before he turns the car off.

"Are you okay?" I ask. I know better than anybody how jealousy can feel. And it doesn't feel good.

"Oh, yeah," says Dad. "I was just thinking about how lucky we are."

"What?"

"All of us. We're setting goals for ourselves, realizing dreams. Spending so much time together as a family. It's a lucky summer. That's what I was thinking about."

Sometimes I don't understand my dad at all.

HEY THERE, POSSUM SAUCE. WHAT'RE YOU THINKING ABOUT?

MAN, IT'S A NICE NIGHT. NOT TOO COLD, NOT TOO HOT. THAT WATER LOOKS GREAT. I ALMOST WISH WE HAD A CAMPFIRE SO WE COULD ROAST SOME HOT DOGS AND MARSHMALLOWS. YOU KNOW WHAT I MEAN? ACTUALLY, WHAT'S STOPPING US?

I'LL HEAD OVER TO THE CANTEEN AND PICK UP SOME PROVISIONS. WHAT *WERE* YOU THINKING ABOUT, ANYWAY?

I WAS THINKING ABOUT HOW MUCH I ENJOYED THE SILENCE.

18

On Saturday morning, Grandma Barrel stands at the kitchen counter, stirring some kind of muffin batter that has raisins and nuts and shreds of carrot in it.

"Aaron has a hard time with a lot of foods, just so you know," I tell her. I slide my mug under the coffee maker and press the button. "It's a *sensory* issue." Mom and Dad have been talking a lot about sensory issues ever since Aaron started therapy.

"Mm-hmm," says Grandma Barrel. She doesn't look up from the mixing bowl.

"He doesn't like foods with little hard pieces in them."

"Mmm."

"He might want to have cereal instead, or—"

"Why don't you let Aaron think for himself, Margaret? He enjoyed my Jell-O." Grandma Barrel looks up at me, but she keeps stirring.

"He *does* think for himself," I say. I feel my cheeks getting hot. "But he needs me to look out for him, too." I splash a little milk into my coffee and put the carton back in the fridge.

Grandma Barrel stops stirring and watches me. "Yes, he does. But he does not need you to discourage him."

"I'm *not* discouraging him!" I squeeze a small dollop of honey into my coffee. An experiment. Maybe it will taste better with honey in it. Grandma Barrel hasn't even been here a whole week. She doesn't know anything about me or Aaron.

"Aaron," Grandma Barrel calls into the living room. Aaron looks up at us over the back of the couch. He has been studying a new list of words he made. "Aaron, dear," she continues. "Would you like to eat Grandma Barrel's famous Morning Glory muffins for breakfast?"

"Yes," says Aaron, in his small, high voice. He disappears behind the couch again.

"Even if they have raisins and nuts and carrots in them?" Grandma Barrel smiles an unpleasant smile at me.

Aaron takes a minute to process what she has asked. "Yes. *Things.*" he says eventually.

"You see?" Grandma Barrel goes back to stirring her muffin batter. "It will be just fine."

I pick my coffee up too fast and slosh a little bit on the counter. I don't care. I take it to my room.

"Margaret," Grandma Barrel calls after me. "If you're old enough to drink coffee, you're old enough to clean up your spill."

I march back into the kitchen. "Comic Con," I whisper, as I wipe up the spilled coffee. "Comic Con, Comic Con, Nora Cho, Comic Con. Junior Forest Ranger Camp." *Don't blow it, Maggie Chowder.* I throw away the paper towel, go back to my room, and close the door. I sit down at my desk and take a sip of my coffee. It is *much* better. Maybe even good.

"Margaret? You really should have used a spray. The counter feels tacky," I hear Grandma Barrel call again.

"I know, Grandma Barrel. I'll clean it up in a minute," I yell.

Comic Con, Comic Con, Nora Cho, Comic Con. I take another sip.

When I come out of my room an hour later, there is a basket of hot muffins on the table. Mom is at the table alone, eating one with her coffee. Grandma Barrel and Aaron are on the couch watching *Diagnosis Murder* with a TV tray in front of them.

Grandma Barrel raises an eyebrow at me. "This is Aaron's third muffin! Can you believe that? His third!" She smiles charmingly at Aaron. "You love Grandma's baking, don't you, Aaron?"

"Yes," says Aaron.

I sit down at the table across from Mom.

"Good morning," I say.

"Good morning." She yawns. "Grandma Barrel let me sleep in a little this morning. Isn't that nice?"

"Sure," I say.

"Your dad left to tape *Lyle* at three o'clock in the morning. They're taping a nighttime episode." She takes a sip of coffee. "He should be home soon. Let's talk about your Seahawks practice tomorrow."

"Okay."

"I am counting on you to be responsible," she says. She looks tired, and her face is very serious.

"I know," I say.

"I'll pack Aaron's noise-canceling headphones in the bag. If it gets too loud or chaotic, he can use those."

"Okay."

"I'll pack Goldfish crackers and apple slices in case either of you wants a snack. I'll pack a book in case he needs to check out and decompress, and I'll pack the emergency phone in case anything happens."

The emergency phone is a prepaid family cell phone that I'm never actually allowed to use. It only has my mom's number in the contact list, and it's only for stuff like this.

"Nothing is going to happen," I say.

"Maggie, I need to know that you'll call me if anything does happen." Mom's face isn't as freckly as it used to be, either. I wonder if stress makes freckles disappear.

"I will," I say.

The front door opens, and Dad walks in. He looks tired and happy. He's carrying his crocodile snout in his arms like it's a baby. Mom rushes to the door and kisses him. I get up and give him a hug.

"How did it go?" Mom asks.

"*Amazingly*. It went amazingly. The cast has such great chemistry, and the script is so good. Oh! Everybody is going to come over on premiere day to watch the first episode. I hope that's okay. They're all such great people. I'm really lucky to get to act with them. The whole thing feels like a dream. Why didn't I get laid off and take up acting sooner?"

Grandma Barrel pokes her head over the back of the couch and looks at Dad. "Because you needed to make actual money to feed your family and pay your mortgage."

Dad leans in close to Mom and whispers, "Even Barrel can't ruin my day." Then he says louder, "Hiya, Barrel. I didn't see you there. Aaron, come give your favorite actor a hug!"

Aaron pokes his head over the back of the couch, too. "My favorite actor is Dick Van Dyke."

Dick Van Dyke is an actor from *Diagnosis Murder*.

"Come give your dad a hug, then," says Dad.

Aaron hurries over to Dad and hugs him. "Today I am watching TV with Grandma Barrel. Tomorrow I am going to a Seahawks practice with Maggie."

"You're right, buddy!" says Dad. "Are you excited?"

Aaron doesn't answer. He goes back to the couch and sits down.

"How about you, Maggie? Are *you* excited?" Dad asks.

"Yeah," I say. I'm excited. I like the Seahawks. And I like LaTanya. But I can't stop thinking about her beautiful house and her mom's glamorous commercial crew, and it's hard not to compare all of her awesome stuff with my not-at-all awesome stuff. And I'm a little worried about people there not understanding some of Aaron's autism stuff, like when he repeats stuff and makes lists and yells.

At least I'll get to show Mom and Dad that I can handle watching Aaron and doing responsible things away from them. Like Comic Con, and maybe—possibly—*some*day, Junior Forest Ranger Camp.

I get kind of shivery every time I think about meeting Nora Cho. Mom registered me and Grandma Barrel for Comic Con last night. Something is *finally* going right this summer.

At the dinner table, Mom and Dad are practicing safety with Aaron.

"What's your phone number, buddy?" asks Dad.

"206-555-0144," says Aaron.

"Who do you ask for help?"

"A grown-up or someone with a badge."

"Great job, buddy," says Mom.

I swallow my bite of chicken. "You guys know I'll be there with him. I won't let him out of my sight, I promise."

"We know you're going to do a great job, Maggie, but just in case—"

"You don't need a *just in case*! I can do this."

"Just in case," continues Mom, "I want Aaron to know his number, where he lives, our names, and what to do if he gets lost. These are really good things for him to know. We'll be having lunch somewhere nearby, too. In case you need us. Grandma Barrel will be here at home. You'll be able to reach all of us. Just in case."

I KNOW YOU'RE SCARED. I KNOW YOU'VE BEEN LOST IN THE WOODS FOR DAYS. BUT YOU'RE SAFE NOW.

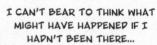

I'M GOING TO FIND YOUR FAMILY, AND I'M GOING TO BRING YOU HOME.

I'M JUST GLAD *I'M* THE ONE WHO FOUND HIM. TERRIBLE THINGS LURK IN THESE WOODS.

I CAN'T BEAR TO THINK WHAT MIGHT HAVE HAPPENED IF I HADN'T BEEN THERE...

19

We are ready to go early in the morning on Sunday. We're both wearing blue and green Seahawks shirts, and Aaron is carrying his newest list of words.

"Do you want to stick your list in the bag Mom packed for you, Aaron?" I ask.

"No," says Aaron. After the incident where I accidentally ripped his list, he doesn't trust me with them.

Mom rushes into the dining room with a rolled-up fleece blanket in her arms. "Take this. I don't want you to get cold." She crams it into the tote bag that's already too full. "And, Aaron, why don't you use the bathroom one more time before you leave."

"LaTanya's going to be here in a minute," I say.

"That's okay," Mom says. "They can come up for a few minutes."

I get a sinking feeling in my stomach. I don't want

LaTanya and her mom to come up for a few minutes. Especially now that they have a big new house. Especially now that we have Grandma Barrel. Especially now that Grandma Barrel got up early to make some kind of cabbage and beef soup in the Crock-Pot, and it smells awful.

I watch from the window that looks out over the apartment complex's parking lot. A big pearly-white SUV with a Seahawks flag waving from the top pulls up and parks, and I know it's LaTanya's mom.

"Mom, they're here!" I yell.

"There's no rush," Mom yells back. "Aaron is washing his hands. Let them in if they knock."

Dad walks over to the window and puts his hands on my shoulders. "*Wow*. Do you smell that? It smells fantastic. Say what you will about your grandma Barrel, but she makes a great-smelling cabbage soup."

I look up at him. There is green face paint all along his hairline and on his chin.

"Dad, you're still green," I say.

"Am I?" He scratches his chin but doesn't make a move toward the bathroom to wash his face.

I look out the window again and see LaTanya and her mom climbing out of the pearly-white SUV.

"Aaron, hurry up!" I yell.

"Hey, hey, don't hurry him," says Dad. "What are you

so anxious about? I thought you said you could handle looking after your brother today."

"I can! I just…I don't want to be late. I don't want to
miss anything." I bite the inside of my cheek. I can't tell
Dad that I'm ashamed of our family and our apartment.
Especially after his *I was just thinking about how lucky we are*
speech from the other night.

I can't see LaTanya and her mom anymore. They must
be on the stairs.

"Aaron!" I yell.

Aaron pads down the hallway clutching his list. "My list
is wet," he says.

"Okay, well, we have to go." I hoist the heavy tote bag
onto my shoulder and start to turn the doorknob.

"My list is wet," he says again. He's standing now, looking at his list. "It's wet."

Mom hurries down the hallway after him. "Sorry, buddy,
that's just from washing your hands. It'll dry." She kisses him
on top of his head.

"My list." Aaron looks up from his list, and his eyes are
full of tears.

"Aaron, *please*," I say. Everything is going wrong. He's
going to have a tantrum, and the apartment smells worse
every second. I can hear footsteps on the stairs, and Dad's
face still looks reptiley.

"My *list*." Aaron's mouth is a perfect frown. He closes his eyes, and big tears roll down his cheeks.

Knock, knock.

My face is hot, and my body feels weird and tight.

Knock, knock.

"Maggie, that's your friend. Are you going to answer the door?" Dad asks. He and Mom are staring at me. Grandma Barrel pokes her head over the back of the couch. Her hair is in green spongy curlers. Aaron is still crying with his eyes closed.

I close my eyes, too. I swing open the door and show LaTanya and her mom all of the most embarrassing things in my life.

"Maggie, look at you! I didn't even get a chance to see you when you were over the other day. I feel like you've grown two inches since the last time I saw you!" I open one eye as I feel LaTanya's mom wrap me up in a big hug. "Are you excited to watch some football?"

I open my other eye and nod.

LaTanya looks behind me at Aaron. "Oh no, is Aaron sad?"

"He has a list of words he wrote down, but it got wet," Mom says. "He was hoping to bring it with him." She ruffles Aaron's hair.

"Well, we're in no rush," says LaTanya's mom.

"Aaron, would you like to write another list?"

Aaron opens his eyes. His frown gets smaller. "Yes," he says after a few seconds.

Mom ushers Aaron back into our room so he can write another list.

"Come in," says Dad. "Have a seat! Would you like coffee? Water?"

"Oh, we're fine," says LaTanya's mom. "Now, this must be Grandma Barrel! It's a pleasure to meet you, ma'am," she says to Grandma Barrel, who has just realized her curlers are still in.

"Yes, it's a pleasure to meet you, too," says Grandma Barrel. She joins us all at the table, unwinding green curlers. I can tell that she is impressed by LaTanya's mom. Everyone is impressed by LaTanya's mom. A real-life Dahlia, Queen Warrior. She also looks like an actress. But a real actress. Not a *Lyle, Lyle Crocodile* actress.

"I'll have to leave the kids alone for the first hour of practice to do press. I hope that's alright." LaTanya's mom smiles apologetically at Dad.

"I suppose that's alright," says Dad. "Maggie keeps telling us she can take care of Aaron." He winks at me. "Press! Wow! And you shot that landscaping commercial, too. I guess you're seeing a lot of cameras these days, huh?"

"Oh, yes. It's been quite a whirlwind!" says LaTanya's mom.

"I bet! You know, I've been spending some time in front of the cameras lately, myself."

I get that hot, uncomfortable feeling again. "I'm going to check on Aaron," I say. As I walk down the hallway, I hear Dad telling LaTanya's mom about his web series.

"Hey, wait up," says LaTanya. She pushes her chair back and follows me to my room. Aaron is at the desk, looking over his new list.

"P-I-C-K spells 'pick,'" says Aaron.

"Wow, he's a really smart four-year-old," says LaTanya. Mom is crouched down next to Aaron's chair. She looks up and smiles at LaTanya.

"G-I-V-E spells 'give,'" says Aaron.

"Aaron, why don't you spell your new word for them?" says Mom.

"S-E-A-H-A-W-K-S spells 'Seahawks,'" says Aaron.

"He-ey," LaTanya says, "you have to spell that for my dad when you see him, Aaron! That's amazing!"

Aaron looks at LaTanya. His cheeks are pink, and he is clearly pleased with himself.

"A-M-A-Z-I-N-G spells 'amazing,'" says Aaron.

"Oh, man. You really are amazing." LaTanya shakes her head in disbelief. We walk back to the dining area together. "You know what else is amazing? That smell. What is that? Soup? It's making me hungry."

THERE ARE HORRIBLE, BEASTLY SOUNDS COMING FROM INSIDE THE CAVE BY WHISPER LAKE. WOULD YOU CHECK ON THAT? AND EAGIRL—BE CAREFUL.

WHAT KIND OF ANIMAL MAKES THOSE—

...SOUNDS?

20

There aren't any bleachers at the Seahawks practice field. We spread out the blanket Mom packed us on the hill behind a whole family of people wearing shaggy blue-and-green wigs.

"If you're all settled, I need to run inside for a couple of press interviews. Are you kids okay here for a little bit?" LaTanya's mom pulls a pair of gold sunglasses from her purse and puts them on. She looks out at the water past the playing field. "Isn't it beautiful? That's Lake Washington right there."

It is beautiful. The sun sparkles on top of the lake, and evergreen trees spread out green and lush behind it. On the field in front of us, some of the Seahawks players are running out, shaking hands and giving high fives to the fans closest to them.

LaTanya's mom wiggles her fingers in a wave and heads into the big building behind us.

I stretch my legs out and lean back on my elbows. The sun feels good. Sometimes in Washington it feels like the sun will never come out, but here it is. I look over at Aaron. He has already pulled out the book Mom packed. He begins reading loudly, clearly, and slowly.

"'Sammy was a fish.'"

"Hey, Aaron," I say, leaning closer to him. "Maybe you could read a little quieter? Or just in your head?"

Aaron looks up at me, then to the side, as though he is considering what I said.

"'Sammy was a fish,'" he begins again, just as loud.

I groan.

"'He liked to swim, and he liked to play.'"

"Wow," says LaTanya. "Is he *reading* that? I know he can spell, but he's reading? That's really cool."

I guess it is. But it doesn't feel cool when he's doing it so loudly, and in front of a whole bunch of strangers who are just trying to watch the Seahawks practice. They probably paid a lot of money to be here. They probably don't want a four-year-old kid belting out the story of Sammy the fish.

"Aaron," I say again. "Can you read that just in your head? Please?"

Aaron looks up at me. He furrows his little forehead. Then he looks back down at his book. "'Sammy was a fish. He liked to swim, and he liked to play.'"

"Aaron!" I say, a little snappier than I mean to. "All done with the book, okay? Can we please all just watch the practice? Look! There's Blitz over there! You love Blitz." I point to the far side of the field, where Blitz the mascot is flapping his wings and dancing in a circle with a group of kids in Seahawks jerseys.

Aaron looks over at Blitz and seems momentarily transfixed. I sneak the book away from him and tuck it back into the bag.

"Hey!" LaTanya stands up. "That's my dad!"

LaTanya's dad walks onto the field with the head coach. A few people clap, but LaTanya jumps up and down and yells.

"YEAH! Go, Dad! Wooo!"

Mr. Richards hears her, turns to us, and blows LaTanya a kiss.

LaTanya sits down. Her face is beaming with pride. "He didn't get to be home with us that much during the season when he was coaching in Canada," she says. "And I didn't get to go to very many of his games. He's still not home very much, but now I'll at least get to see his games."

I hadn't really thought about that. LaTanya must have missed her dad a lot when he was in Canada without her and her mom.

Loud music blasts from the speakers on both ends of

the field, and the quarterback walks out onto the field. Everybody stands up, yelling and clapping. The quarterback waves to us and motions for the Seahawks to gather up in the middle of the field. Blitz runs to the middle of the field, too, acting like he's going to be part of the game.

I look down at Aaron to see if he's still watching, but Aaron isn't there.

My chest gets tight, and I feel like all of the air is suddenly sucked out of me.

"Aaron," I squeak.

"What?" LaTanya turns to me. "What did you… Where's Aaron?" She realizes he's gone. "Maggie, where's—"

"I don't know!" I search the ground between blankets, looking all over the hill. I don't see Aaron. He isn't anywhere.

"We have to get help," LaTanya says. "We need to ask security to help. They'll make an announcement, and then everyone can help us look—"

"No!" My heart is beating out of my chest. "We don't need to get security. I can handle this. I can find Aaron." This is what I was *born* for. Aaron needs me, and I'm going to find him. "C'mon." I pull LaTanya by the wrist up the hill.

"Where are we going?" she asks.

"We'll be able to see more ground from the top of the hill. If we can't find him that way, we'll get into the building and head to the top floor. We'll find a window that will give us the best vantage point." Like a forest ranger's lookout tower. I can do this.

"Maggie, we have to find my mom. She's inside. Let's tell her what happened. She'll be able to help! She can—"

"No!" I say again. If we tell LaTanya's mom that Aaron disappeared, she'll just call my parents. They'll never trust me again, and anyway, I know I can find him without grown-ups getting involved. That's what Eagirl would do.

I pull LaTanya to the top of the hill, and I scan everything below us. The hundreds of people in folding chairs and on blankets, and the players on the field. There's no Aaron.

We head into the building and run past an enormous gym with rows and rows of treadmills and weight benches. There's an elevator at the other end of the ground floor, and I press the highest number it will go. We get in and wait what seems like forever for the doors to close, lift us several floors, and open again. When they do, we run out into a long hallway with big windows.

"Here!" I say. "We can see everything from here."

I stand there with LaTanya for a very long time in

silence. At first, we're silent because we are searching for Aaron. After a while, we are silent because we really can't find him. And we've looked for several minutes. And it's starting to seem really, really hopeless. Aaron isn't there.

21

After what seems like half an hour, LaTanya and I take the elevator back to the ground floor in silence. I don't have any more ideas. I don't know how to find my brother. He must be so scared, and it's all my fault. I wasn't paying attention. I took his book away, so he must have gotten upset or bored, and he left. It's my fault.

The elevator door dings open, and we step out. Maybe Aaron has gotten into the building, too. Maybe that's why we couldn't see him from the windows on the top floor.

"Let's check the gym," I say.

LaTanya nods. Her face is stricken. She looks the way I feel.

We search the exercise equipment, checking underneath benches and behind machines. There is a locker room attached, so we check that, too. We open every locker. We check every shower and every bathroom stall.

"Maggie," LaTanya says, "I think we need to find help."

I don't want to agree with LaTanya, but I do. I messed up, and I can't fix it.

The locker-room door squeaks open. LaTanya and I look at each other.

"Hello?" I call. "Aaron?"

I hear rustling as someone moves closer to the row of lockers we're standing next to. My heart feels just a little lighter. Just a little hopeful.

A large man with a walkie-talkie and a flashlight steps in front of us.

"What are you two doing here? You're not supposed to be in here!" he says.

"We're looking for my brother," I tell him. I nearly choke on my sentence because I am so sad and so worried and also a little relieved that there is an adult here who can maybe help us. "We lost him. Maybe thirty minutes ago. Maybe more."

The man tilts his head back and looks at me carefully. "Your brother? He a little boy? Doesn't say much?"

Hot tears flood my eyes. "Yes! That's Aaron. Do you have him?"

The man nods. "Follow me."

We follow him out of the locker room and gym, down two hallways, and to a little room with a glass window. The door says SECURITY. Through the window, I see Aaron sitting down at a card table with his Sammy the fish book. For a moment, I feel nothing but relief, because he's okay. He's safe. Then, I realize I am in the biggest trouble of my entire life. I know this, because right behind Aaron are my mom and dad. And they are staring at me through the window like they are *furious*. LaTanya's mom is standing next to them, shaking her head at us. I've never seen LaTanya's mom look mad before, but she is definitely mad now.

The man opens the door and motions to me. "These the girls you're looking for?" he asks our parents.

"Oh, yeah," says Mom. "These are the girls."

The man nods and motions for me and LaTanya to step inside. "I'll leave you folks alone to talk for a few minutes."

He closes the door behind us, and all of the parents begin to talk at once.

"What were you thinking?" says LaTanya's mom. "I went back to the blanket after my interviews, and you were all gone! Just disappeared!"

"Margaret Michelle Chowder," says Mom. "You *promised* me you would look after Aaron. You promised. You said you would call us on the emergency phone if anything happened. We were at the diner, right across the street. We would have been here in five minutes."

"Why was Aaron by himself?" asks Dad. "Do you

know what could have happened to him? *Anything* could have happened to him!"

I look down at my shoes. Big, fat tears roll out of my eyes and onto the tops of them. I can hear LaTanya sniffling next to me, too.

"I'm sorry," I say. "I'm so, so sorry. I made the wrong choice. Aaron was gone all of a sudden, and I thought I could find him by myself, but I should have found an adult. I should have asked for help." I tried to be like Eagirl and save Aaron myself. You know, *bring protection to all creatures*. That's what she does. But Eagirl isn't too proud to ask for help when she needs it. Eagirl never would have done what I did.

"Yeah, you should have," says Mom. "Thank goodness Aaron did."

I look up at her. "He did?"

"Yes. He found a security guard with a badge and gave him our names and phone number."

I look at Aaron. He is looking at his book, but I see him smile just slightly. He knows he did the right thing.

"He wandered away because of me," I say. "He was reading his book out loud, and I thought he was bothering people, so I packed it back up. I'm sorry. I'm really sorry, Aaron. That wasn't nice."

Aaron looks up at me.

"No, it wasn't nice," Mom says. "I'm so disappointed in you I could just cry, Maggie."

I feel like my heart is made of lead. "Can we go home?" I ask.

"Yeah, I think that's a good idea," says Dad. "C'mon, buddy," he says to Aaron. "Let's go home."

"Let's go home," echoes Aaron.

"I'm sorry, LaTanya. I'm sorry, Mrs. Richards. I was really irresponsible." I run my sleeve across my nose, because I don't see any tissues anywhere, and I don't feel like asking for one.

"I'm just glad it all turned out okay, honey," says LaTanya's mom.

"See you soon?" asks LaTanya. I nod my head, but I don't actually know if I will see her soon. I'm probably grounded until college, and even if I'm not, I don't know that I want to see anyone for a long time. I let everybody down. Aaron could have been kidnapped, or run onto the road, or…Anything could have happened. And it would have been my fault.

22

I never want to leave my bedroom again. Or my bed, for
that matter. I have Anderson Cooper and a stack of Eagirl
comics under the covers with me, but I can't even bother to
read them. I'm nothing like Eagirl. She's brave and smart
and would *never* break the rules just to avoid getting in trouble. She would have radioed Ranger Danger immediately
if her little brother went missing. Actually, she probably
wouldn't have had to. She never would have made her
brother go missing in the first place. She would never have
taken his book away.

Aaron wasn't hurting anyone. He was just reading. Why
was I so embarrassed? Why am I always so embarrassed?
Aaron's just fine. I'm the one who doesn't make good
choices. And I'm the one everybody's mad at.

Our bedroom door opens, and I look down to see who
it is. Aaron.

"Hi, buddy," I say.

He looks up at me. "Hi, buddy," he says back.

"I'm sorry about everything, Aaron." I feel more tears fill my eyes. "I wasn't a very good sister to you today, huh?"

Aaron sits down on his bed, where I can't see him. I roll over and close my eyes.

"I'll be better. I'll never let you get lost again. I'll never take your book away. I'll do better."

I don't hear anything.

"Okay?" I ask.

" 'Sammy was a fish,' " Aaron says. I hear the sound of a page turning. " 'He liked to swim, and he liked to play.' "

✖✖✖

I must have fallen asleep while Aaron was reading his book. When I wake up, it's light outside. Aaron is gone, and I hear clinking silverware on dishes at the table. I don't want to see or talk to anyone, but my stomach growls, and I realize I didn't eat dinner last night.

I climb down from the top bunk with my blanket wrapped around my shoulders like a shawl. I pad down the hallway and into the dining area. Everyone looks up at me.

"Good morning, honey," says Mom.

The last time I saw her, she was so mad at me. And so disappointed. But she doesn't look mad or disappointed now.

"Good morning!" says Dad.

I half smile at them both and wave from under my blanket shawl.

"Coffee?" asks Dad. He gestures to his coffee cup.

"Okay," I shrug.

"The counter is still sticky from your spill yesterday. You really should have used a spray," Grandma Barrel says, raising her eyebrows as she sips her own coffee.

I stare at her.

"We all have responsibilities, Margaret," she says. "The coffee spill is *your* responsibility."

My stomach growls again, but I don't care. I go back to my room and close the door. I crawl into my bunk and pull the covers up over my head.

"Ma," I hear Mom say in the other room. "This wasn't the time."

I hear more clinking.

Then I hear footsteps. And two loud knocks on my door.

"I come bearing food!" It's Dad.

"Come in," I mumble from under my blankets.

Dad comes in and hands me a plate of toast with butter and jelly on it.

"Thanks," I say.

"You're very welcome. Your coffee will be done in a minute. Milk?"

"And honey," I say.

I hear Dad sit down on Aaron's bed. "It's okay to be sad, Maggie."

"I know," I say. I don't know why, but my voice sounds trembly when it comes out.

"You made a mistake. A *big* mistake. And it could have had terrible consequences. *But* you learned from it. And everything is okay. Better than okay. It's pretty great, all things considered. We found out that Aaron can handle a scary situation."

"And that I can't." My gut tightens up, and it feels like there's cotton in my throat. I stare warily at my toast. I'm hungry, but I don't know how I could possibly swallow.

"You can, Maggie. You were born to handle scary situations. You'll have other chances to prove yourself. And hey, I'm sorry about your grandmother. She's…"

"Yeah, I know," I say.

"But she's also been talking nonstop about Comic Con. She's excited to hang out with you, Mags."

I think about the bumpy, bunched-up seams I sewed in Grandma Barrel's Possum Sauce costume.

Dad stands up. "I'll go get your coffee. Why don't you read some Eagirl comics? Have your breakfast, spend some time thinking, and maybe forgive yourself. You're a really great kid."

Forgive myself. I'm not so sure I can.

I take Aaron's sensory bottle from under the bed, where he left it. I turn it upside down and watch the glitter, beads, and pipe-cleaner pieces fall gently to the bottom.

23

I spend most of the next few days reading in my room. But not just Eagirl comics. I read the old books Grandma Barrel gave to me. The ones that were in the suitcase. There's one on foraging in the Pacific Northwest, one about wildlife preservation, and one called *Law Enforcement in Forestry: The Forest Ranger's Handbook.* It has all kinds of good ranger rules. *Assess the situation. Know when to call for help.* The handbook is very clear: a forest ranger must follow protocol. If they don't, they can put countless lives in danger.

I didn't follow protocol with Aaron at the Seahawks practice. I broke the rules and tried to do it my way, and that was the wrong way. I didn't really assess the situation. I didn't know when to call for help.

I worry that I can't trust my instincts, because my instincts were so wrong. And instincts are a forest ranger's most important asset. Instincts and rules. Instincts and rules are the difference between campfires and wildfires. Instincts and rules save lives and miles of trees. But my instincts don't seem to work, and I ignored the rules.

"Maggie!" I hear Dad call from the kitchen. "LaTanya is on the phone for you!"

I start to close my copy of *Law Enforcement in Forestry*. Before the cover snaps shut all the way, I see something scrawled in pen across the title page. I open the book again. Right above the bold title of the book, someone has written *Barrel Parry.* Barrel! This was Grandma Barrel's book. Why did Grandma Barrel have a forest ranger's handbook?

"Maggie!" Dad calls again.

I close the book and leave it on my bed. A mystery to solve later.

I haven't talked to LaTanya since the Seahawks practice.

When I get to the kitchen, I take the phone from Dad. "Hello?"

"Maggie! It's been like forty-thousand years! How are you? Are your parents still mad at you? I miss you! Can I come sleep over at your house tonight?"

I take the phone back to my room. "My house? It's not even a house. It's an apartment. Why don't we sleep over at *your* house?"

"Because my dad has to get up early tomorrow for

practice and my mom has the cleaners here all day, and I have to stay out of their way. Plus, I *like* your apartment."

I look around my bedroom. Aaron's lists are lined up across my desk, and Anderson Cooper is stolen again, tucked half under Aaron's pillow. His blankets are only partially on the bed. There is a falling-over stack of Eagirl comics on the floor by the bunk bed, and a very long row of Aaron's trains stretching from the far wall to the door. It must be nice to have cleaners.

"Let me ask my dad," I say.

I bring the phone back to the kitchen.

"Can LaTanya sleep over tonight?"

"Yes! That's a great idea! The first episode of *Lyle, Lyle Crocodile* will be available to watch at seven. The whole cast is coming over, remember? We'll make it a real screening party! Tell LaTanya to wear her greenest pajamas."

I sigh. I put the phone back up to my ear. "Did you catch that?"

"My greenest pajamas. I'll wear 'em! My mom will drop me off around dinnertime. See you then!"

LaTanya hangs up.

I'm a little worried about what Dad's *Lyle, Lyle Crocodile* screening party will look like, but I'm also excited for LaTanya to sleep over and for things to feel back to normal, kind of.

At four, Mom is home from work. Her braid is sweaty, and her work shirt has an orange stain on it, but she hums around the kitchen anyway, rolling out a blob of pizza dough she brought home from her market.

"Can I put the sauce and cheese on?" I ask. That's my favorite part. And anyway, I am trying to show everyone that I can help. I can still do things without messing them up.

"Sure, honey," says Mom. She slides the jar of pizza sauce over to me, and I spoon it onto the dough, spreading it almost all the way to the edges.

"How was work?" I ask. I don't know very much about my mom's job. I know she has some bad days, and Grandma Barrel doesn't like the job that much. But I don't really know anything else.

"You know, it was a pretty good day," says Mom. "A really good day, actually. Our head baker quit. I had to fill in for him."

"Oh," I say. "I'm sorry he quit."

"I'm not," says Mom. "I loved every minute of working in the bakery."

"Cool," I say. "I'm glad."

Mom really does seem happier than usual. Maybe she's mastered *The Art of Being Okay When You're Not Okay*. Maybe she's really okay now.

The clock on the oven catches her eye, and she startles. "Oh! It's four. Your brother's sweet new friend is coming over for an hour before dinner."

"Aaron has a friend?" I say, and then I realize.

Knock, knock. Knockknockknockknockknockknock.

Mom runs to the front door.

"Hello, there! You must be Eva!" Mom says.

"I know that," says Eva.

I get a familiar tight feeling in my stomach. Eva from Aaron's therapy. The one who accused me of *bumping* her. Great.

Eva wanders into the kitchen. She stretches on her tiptoes to see what I'm sprinkling on the pizza.

"I don't like cheese," she says.

"That's fine," I say, "because you definitely aren't staying for dinner."

"I don't like sauce, either," she says. "Where's Aaron?"

I hear Mom talking quietly with Eva's mom at the door.

"Aaron is watching *Diagnosis Murder* in the living room with Grandma Barrel," I say. I point to the couch on the far end of the living room, where Aaron and Grandma Barrel both poke their heads over the back of the couch.

"I don't like cheese and sauce," Eva calls to Aaron.

Aaron grins. "I like cheese and sauce," he calls back.

Eva joins Aaron and Grandma Barrel on the couch in front of *Diagnosis Murder*.

Mom closes the door and joins me in the kitchen again.

"I think she is just the sweetest thing," Mom says in a quiet voice.

I bet she won't think so for very long.

HERE SHE IS, EAGIRL! YOUR NEW PUPIL. YOUR PROTÉGÉ. YOUR FUTURE SIDEKICK.

WELL, I, UH... NICE TO MEET YOU, KID. BUT I'VE GOT A SIDEKICK. HER NAME IS POSSUM SAUCE. I'M SURE I CAN TEACH YOU A FEW THINGS, ANYWAY. WHAT'S YOUR NAME?

THE NAME'S BOSSTRICH. AND SOMEDAY YOU'RE GONNA BE MY SIDEKICK.

YOU KNOW WHAT? I LIKE YOU. OKAY, FIRST THINGS FIRST. WE'RE GOING TO NEED TO DO SOMETHING ABOUT THAT COSTUME.

24

LaTanya arrives at five sharp, wearing green pajamas that have sequins all over them and her V-E-R-Y-B-E-S-T bracelet. She twirls around slowly in the doorway, so I get the full experience.

"Wow," I say. "You really did wear your greenest pajamas."

"The greenest and the sparkliest," LaTanya says. "Hey, who's that?"

I turn my head to look, but I already know who she's talking about. Eva is watching LaTanya from the couch. "That's Aaron's friend, Eva," I say. "She's from Aaron's therapy place."

"No, I'm not," yells Eva. "I'm from Kent, Washington."

LaTanya tries to hide a smile. "Well it's nice to meet you, Eva from Kent, Washington."

"I don't like cheese and sauce," Eva says. She turns

back around to watch *Diagnosis Murder* with Aaron and Grandma Barrel.

"She's not staying for dinner," I tell LaTanya.

But by 5:45 p.m., Eva is still in our apartment, and it's time for dinner.

Mom rolls her pizza cutter through the pizza. "Eva's mom might be a little late. She's running some errands, and I told her to take her time. I said we'd feed Eva if she wasn't back by dinnertime."

Eva walks through the kitchen and peeks at the pizza on tiptoes. "I don't like cheese and sauce."

"Honey," Mom says to me. "Would you fix Eva a plate of *things*?"

"What's *things*?" asks Eva.

I didn't want Eva to stay for dinner. But I open cabinets and the fridge, and I pull out things that aren't cheese or sauce.

"Today, *things* is apple slices, almond butter, Goldfish crackers, and carrot sticks," I say.

Eva is quiet for a moment. "Okay," she says finally. "I like *things*."

We all eat together at the table: me, LaTanya, Mom, Dad, Grandma Barrel, Aaron, and Eva. Aaron chews his pizza thoughtfully. He smiles his biggest smile at Eva.

"I like cheese and sauce," he says.

"I *don't* like cheese and sauce," says Eva. But she's smiling too. She pops a Goldfish cracker into her mouth.

"I *like* cheese and sauce."

"I *don't* like cheese and sauce!"

Aaron and Eva giggle wildly together.

"This is nice," says Grandma Barrel. "A nice dinner."

And it is.

Until Dad looks at the time on his phone. "Six! The premiere is in an hour." He jumps to his feet and jams the end of a pizza crust into his mouth. "I have a few things to set up before the cast gets here." He wiggles his fingers mysteriously at us.

I forgot his *Lyle, Lyle* friends were coming over. Our apartment is small as it is. And there are already three extra people in it! I look around and get that familiar embarrassed feeling all over again. Aaron has a smear of pizza sauce on his cheek. Mom is still wearing her stained work shirt. LaTanya is wearing her sparkliest and greenest pajamas. She looks like an out-of-place princess at bedtime. Heat creeps up my neck and into my face. I close my eyes. I picture Aaron's sensory bottle, with all of the tiny pieces falling slowly to the bottom.

"You okay?" LaTanya whispers.

"Yeah." I open my eyes again. "I'm fine."

Mom starts piling empty plates on top of one another. "I'm so proud of your dad, Maggie. I can't wait to see what he's been working on."

"Mmm. Yes, I'm sure it's going to be an entertaining night," says Grandma Barrel. She rolls her eyes just slightly to one side and takes a sip of water.

Dad reappears with two large rolls of green crepe paper in his hands and a roll of tape in his mouth. He starts unrolling one of the crepe paper rolls.

"Let's go hang out on the balcony," I say to LaTanya. "So we're not in the way."

We aren't really in the way. But I hate that panicky, embarrassed feeling I keep getting. And I need some air.

I pull open the sliding door to the balcony, and LaTanya and I step out. The balcony is my favorite part of our apartment. It's the closest thing we have to a yard. I breathe in, deep. Today, the balcony mostly doesn't smell like garbage from the dumpster. It depends on which way the wind is blowing. Today it smells fresh and green and sweet, because of the giant tangle of invasive blackberry vines on the hill just beyond.

I sit down in one of the two deck chairs, and LaTanya sits in the other. We look out at the blackberries for a long, quiet moment.

"Things are different now," LaTanya says.

She isn't looking at me—she is still facing the blackberry hill—but I can see tears in her eyes.

"Yeah," I say. "They are."

Everything is different. The apartment, Aaron, my parents, me. Well, not Aaron. He's the same, I guess. Anyway, it was only a matter of time before LaTanya wanted out. She probably just wants to go home.

"I hate my new house," LaTanya says with a sudden sob. She covers her face with her hands. Her fingernails are kind of pinky gold, and there aren't any chips or scratches in her nail polish.

My jaw drops open in surprise, but I close it before she notices.

"Why? What's wrong with it?" I put my arm around her shoulders and squeeze her lightly. "What's wrong?"

LaTanya sniffs and wipes her eyes with her arm. "Nothing. But it's not, like…It's not my *home*."

I get a feeling in my chest like a fist squeezing my heart. Tears that I didn't even know were in my eyes fall out over my cheeks, soaking my shirt and dropping onto my knees.

"I know exactly what that feels like," I say. I can barely get the words out because of how trembly my mouth is and how gaspy my breath is as I cry.

"My dad used to never be home because he was coaching football in Canada. And I missed him all the time. And then he got hired by the Seahawks and my mom kept saying he was going to be home with us all the time, but he *never is*!" LaTanya's mouth is trembling, too. "I never see him.

He's always at practice or doing press or traveling. And my mom's technically home, but she's got a *glam squad* and a crew with her all the time.

"Nobody remembers I'm there. They step on my dog and make a mess in the kitchen, and there are like fifty rooms in the new house, but I'm only ever in my bedroom. It's me and Glitter in there by ourselves all the time. And now I'm here with your family, and everybody is just so *together* and having fun with each other."

I squeeze her shoulders tighter. "I'm sorry," I say. "I'm so sorry." And I am. For so many things. "I didn't know you were sad. I guess I didn't know because I wasn't paying attention. I've been really stuck in my own stuff this summer. We had to move out of our house, and I *loved* our house. There aren't any woods behind our apartment here. There's just…" I wave my hand toward the blackberry vines. "And I messed up so bad with Aaron at the Seahawks practice. *So* bad.

"Everything is different in my family. Mom works, and Dad stays home, when he's not…being a crocodile? I don't have my own room anymore. I tried to be okay with everything, but sometimes I feel so sad, it's like I'm at the bottom of a mudslide, like in that Exceptional Eagirl issue. I'm trying to climb out, and I can't. I keep messing things up, when I'm supposed to be the one who fixes things, or who at least doesn't make them worse."

LaTanya squeezes me back. "You aren't Eagirl, you know. You're Maggie Chowder. It's okay to mess up sometimes. And you've got me." Her voice is still unsteady. "We'll climb out of the mud together."

We look out in silence again for a little while. I concentrate on getting my breathing back to normal, and I can hear LaTanya doing the same thing, taking one slow, shaky breath after another.

FROM *THE EXCEPTIONAL EAGIRL #48*

25

When the *Lyle, Lyle* actors arrive for the screening party, they aren't what I expected. I don't know what I did expect, but they aren't it. They aren't like anybody I've ever met. There is a man who kind of looks like Grizzly Baird—handsome and big—and Dad introduces him to Mom as Dag Janssen.

"The pleasure is all mine," Dag says, and he picks up Mom's hand and kisses it.

"Oh, jeez," Mom says, taking her hand back. Her face is pink: she looks embarrassed and happy at the same time.

"Dag plays Mr. Primms," says Dad.

In *Lyle, Lyle, Crocodile*, Mr. Primms and his family move into the brownstone where Lyle, the crocodile, already lives.

There is a woman who has the blondest hair I've ever seen in my whole life. She is wearing a green cocktail dress with tiny beads all over it, and long, fancy green gloves that go all the way up above her elbows. She holds out her hand to me with her fingers pointing down, and I'm worried that she wants me to kiss it like Dag Janssen kissed Mom's hand, but instead she leans way back and says "Absolutely charr-rrmed." She rolls her *r*'s like a cat, but then drops her pose and laughs at her own silliness. "I'm Connie Smolinski. *Mrs. Primms.* Glad to meet you, Maggie. Your dad has told us *so* much about you."

I wonder for a second if Dad has told them about how I lost Aaron at the Seahawks practice.

Dad has set up a couple of folding chairs next to the couch and four pillows on the floor. There are green crepe paper streamers twisted elegantly across the living room and dining area, and bowls of snacks on the table: chips, pista-chios, popcorn, Goldfish crackers, and a veggie tray. *Things.* Aaron will like that.

Dad stands in the middle of the living room with his hands cupped around his green crocodile snout.

"Ladies and gentlemen, in ten minutes, we will begin the premiere of the first episode of *Lyle, Lyle, Crocodile: The Web Series.*"

Connie claps her gloved hands. "I can't wait! We've worked hard, boys. In a few minutes, we'll be *stars.*" She doesn't roll her *r* this time. She pronounces *stars* like it rhymes with *Oz*.

"Ten minutes," says Aaron, curling up on one of the pil-lows on the floor. "It will begin in ten minutes."

"Er, yes," says Connie. "In ten minutes, we'll be *stars*."

Everyone gets comfortable. Eva sits on a pillow next to Aaron. Her mother still hasn't picked her up, but there are so many people in our apartment now that I hardly notice. I sit on another pillow next to LaTanya.

Knock, knock.

Mom answers the door.

"I am *so* sorry I'm this late," I hear Eva's mother say. "I can't thank you enough for keeping her! I got all of my errands done, and I can't remember the last time that happened."

"Anytime at all," Mom says. "And please come in! We're just about to watch the premiere of my husband's web series!"

"Oh my," Eva's mother says. They both join us all in the living room. Mom sits down on a folding chair next to Dad. Out of the corner of my eye, I see her take his crocodile paw and hold it in her hand. My parents are weird, but sometimes they do nice things like that.

Eva's mom sits down between Grandma Barrel and Dag Janssen.

"I'm Pamela Embry," she says, holding her hand out to Dag Janssen like she wants to shake hands.

Dag takes her hand and kisses it just like he did to my mom's. Only Eva's mom doesn't pull her hand away.

"Dag Janssen," says Dag. "Truly, the pleasure is mine.

Nobody told me an angel would be attending our premiere."

"Honestly," says Grandma Barrel. She adjusts her long skirt and looks at the watch on her wrist. "How much longer till this thing starts?"

"Two minutes!" says Dad.

"Were you good for the Chowders?" Eva's mom asks Eva, but she is still looking at Dag Janssen.

"They had pizza for dinner. I don't like sauce and cheese," says Eva.

"Oh, that's nice," says Eva's mom.

Dad clicks on the YouTube app on our TV. He clicks on the *Lyle, Lyle, Crocodile* channel. It's empty so far. There aren't any videos in it yet.

"One minute!" says Dad.

"You could be an actress," Dag Janssen says to Eva's mom. "No, my dear, you *should* be an actress."

LaTanya covers her mouth to keep from laughing.

"Honestly," Grandma Barrel says again.

Most of the time I don't like having a small apartment with small rooms. But tonight, the smallness of the room means we get to hear everything that everyone is saying. I'm glad LaTanya is sleeping over. It means we'll get to talk about it all afterward.

Everyone gasps. A video appears in the *Lyle, Lyle* YouTube channel. It is labeled "Lyle, Lyle, Crocodile: Episode 1."

The thumbnail picture is of Dad, in his full Lyle suit, lying in a bathtub.

"Dad!" says Aaron gleefully, pointing at the TV.

"That's right, buddy!" says Dad. "Here we go!" He clicks the video, and we all watch, transfixed for the whole twelve minutes and seventeen seconds.

When Dad first told us about his web series, I thought it was going to be weird and embarrassing. When he showed us all his crocodile snout, I thought *he* was weird and embarrassing. But the premiere episode of *Lyle, Lyle, Crocodile* is so good, I can't catch my breath the entire time. My chest feels too full of pride to let any air get in.

26

When I wake up the next morning, I have that weird beef-jerky taste in my mouth again. This time I know it's from forgetting to brush my teeth and laughing all night with LaTanya. I hear her stir on the bottom bunk. Aaron is sleeping in Mom and Dad's room to give us privacy.

"*Dahhhling*," says LaTanya, poking her head up next to the top bunk. "You could be an actress. No. You *must* be an actress."

We dissolve into fits of laughter. When the *Lyle* premiere was over last night, Dag Janssen and Eva's mother swapped phone numbers. When Eva's mom typed her number into Dag's phone, he took it back, closed his eyes, and smelled it. LaTanya and I couldn't control ourselves from laughing then, so Mom shooed us off to my room. We stayed up for hours and hours, until the dark sky turned one shade lighter, and we could hear birds chirping to each other. Then we finally fell asleep. It felt just exactly like it used to, before everything changed this summer.

"Last night was so fun. I would *love* to be in a web series someday," says LaTanya.

"You *would?*" I ask. "Like *Lyle?*"

"Yes! I've always wanted to act. Not in commercials like my mom does, but like…real acting. *Web series* acting."

I almost laugh, but don't, because LaTanya isn't joking. And the premiere of Dad's web series was really a lot better than I thought it was going to be.

"Oh, man," says LaTanya. She disappears again, and I hear her sit down on Aaron's bed.

"What?" I sit up.

"I just remembered Comic Con is tomorrow. Are you dressing up?"

I sit up in bed. Tomorrow! I almost forgot. How could I forget? We still have some work to do on our costumes.

"Yes! Grandma Barrel is making my Eagirl costume. And I'm making her costume, too!"

"Your *grandma* is wearing a costume to Comic Con?"

We start laughing again. I can feel the whole bunk bed shaking with our laughter.

"Well, I'm glad I get to be there to see it," says LaTanya.

I wipe a laughter tear from my eye.

Knock, knock, knock.

"Margaret, may I enter?"

Three short, loud knocks and a *Margaret, may I enter* means it's Grandma Barrel.

"Yeah," I say. "Come in!"

Grandma Barrel opens the door.

"Just so you girls are aware, everyone else in this apartment has eaten breakfast. We ate at eight, which is a universally accepted time to eat breakfast. You girls were up laughing all night, and now it is eleven, which is nearly time for lunch. Your mother is at work, and your father is reading his next crocodile script and watching the views go up on his video."

"Thanks, Grandma Barrel. I guess we'll eat lunch, then."

"I can't wait to see your Comic Con costume," says LaTanya. "It's so cool that you're dressing up with Maggie."

Grandma Barrel nods. "Oh yes. Margaret made most of my costume, in fact."

"Most of it?" I ask.

"I like to keep a surprise up my sleeve," says Grandma Barrel. "You'll see it tomorrow. While the two of you were giggling the night away, I finished both of the costumes. They're in the closet. Don't peek at mine." Grandma Barrel walks away, leaving the door open.

"A woman of mystery!" says LaTanya.

"*So* mysterious." I laugh.

LaTanya and I stumble into the kitchen and search the cabinets for food.

"I know it's almost the universally accepted time for lunch," says LaTanya, "but can we have cereal?"

"I think cereal is universally acceptable for all meals. And snacks, too," I say. I pour us each a bowl full.

Aaron is putting together a floor puzzle in the living room. We watch him work while we eat. He carefully scans the puzzle, then picks up a puzzle piece and fits it into its spot.

"I get to be Eagirl tomorrow, Aaron," I say.

Aaron doesn't look up from his puzzle. "I get to be Aaron tomorrow," he says.

I set our cereal bowls on the table, and LaTanya and I sit down.

"Your brother is probably the coolest person out there," says LaTanya.

I smile at her. She's right.

"Are you going to dress up tomorrow?" I ask.

LaTanya sighs. "I have to wear a Seahawks jersey since I'll be hanging out with the Seahawks all day."

"Bummer," I say.

"But I can help with your hair, if you want." She wiggles

her eyebrows at me. "I can give you some Eagirl braids."

I don't know how to braid. I wear my hair in a ponytail most of the time. "I would love that," I say. And I really would.

I jump in the shower after we eat. When I come out of the bathroom, LaTanya is ready with a comb and a couple of hair products in spray bottles.

"These are so your hair lasts till tomorrow."

LaTanya brushes, braids, and sprays my hair, and it reminds me of dozens of sleepovers we've had before. Staying up all night laughing with LaTanya reminded me of them too. I feel lighter today, like maybe everything isn't completely different after all. Some things are, but not everything.

"Ta-da," says LaTanya. "I'm done. What do you think?"

I look in the mirror on my wall.

"It looks *just* like Eagirl's hair. I can't believe it." I put my hand up to feel how crunchy my braids are.

"Hey!" LaTanya whaps my hand gently with the brush. "No touching. These babies have to last till the end of the day tomorrow."

"You're really good at doing hair, LaTanya," I say.

"I know." LaTanya looks at her nails. "I don't need my mom's glam squad. I'm my *own* glam squad."

We both laugh.

I think about my Eagirl costume hanging in the coat closet. I haven't seen it finished yet, but it was already beautiful when it was still missing feathers. I have butterflies in my stomach thinking about tomorrow.

"LaTanya," I say. "I get to meet Nora Cho in like eighteen hours."

LaTanya grabs my hand and we both squeal.

"What are you going to *say* to her?" LaTanya asks.

"Probably…thank you?" I say, laughing. "I love you? You changed my whole life?"

✖✖✖

When Mom gets home from work, she has a couple loaves of bread under her arm and a white stripe of flour across one cheek.

"Oh! Did LaTanya go home already?" she asks.

"Yeah, her mom picked her up an hour ago. Did you work in the bakery again?"

Mom is beaming. She puts the loaves down on the kitchen counter and pulls me into a tight hug. She smells like dough. "I sure did. And I'll work in the bakery tomorrow, and the day after tomorrow, and the day after that. I told my boss how much I've loved taking over for the head baker, and I mentioned my pastry chef experience. You're looking at the new head baker at our grocery store!"

Dad hops over the back of the couch where he was sitting with Aaron. He grabs Mom's face in his hands and kisses her. I look away.

"That is *amazing*," he says. "Congratulations, babe. I knew it. This really is the summer of our dreams coming true."

The summer of our dreams coming true. I don't know about that. But I am really glad my mom is going to be a baker after all.

27

The morning of Comic Con, I don't even need my alarm to wake me up. For one thing, I am so excited to wear my amazing Eagirl costume and meet Nora Cho that I am full of adrenaline. And for another thing, my hair hurts, and my neck is stiff from trying not to wreck my hairstyle all night. But when I sit up and look in the mirror on the wall across the room, it looks exactly like it did yesterday.

I feel around for Anderson Cooper, but he's nowhere. I'm *sure* I had him when I went to sleep last night. I creep down from the top bunk and look at Aaron, who is still sleeping. His little fist is clutching Anderson Cooper's furry neck.

Well played, Aaron, I think. *If you can sneak Anderson Cooper out from under my arm in the middle of the night, you deserve him.* Maybe Aaron will be a spy someday. Or a professional jewel thief.

I open my door quietly so I don't wake Aaron and

retrieve my Eagirl costume from the coat closet. Grandma Barrel's costume is already gone. She must be up already. I change in the bathroom, wash my face in the sink, and when I look in the mirror, my heart thuds inside my chest. I actually look pretty good. I look almost like *Eagirl*. Almost. My hair is great. My costume is basic, but it's also beautiful, and the general idea is right. It's not itchy or too hot. And I can move around in it, which I like. Grandma Barrel sewed dozens of feathers and a belt onto it the other night. Her stitches are all small and perfect.

I smell coffee as soon as I walk out of the bathroom. Mom is in the kitchen, squeezing honey into the PNW mug. She looks up.

"Oh, Maggie," she says. "You look *wonderful*. You truly do look like Eagirl."

I sit down at the table, and she sets the coffee mug in front of me.

"Thanks, Mom."

"Have you seen your grandmother yet this morning?"

"No, I haven't." I look into the living room, but she isn't there.

"She's having her coffee out on the balcony," says Mom. "You should take a look."

I bring my coffee with me. When I slide the balcony door open and step out, I almost drop my mug. Grandma Barrel is sitting in a chair, looking like Possum Sauce's elderly aunt. She is wearing the gray costume I made her, bumpy seams, uneven stitches, and all. But my bad sewing actually kind of *works*. It looks like it was on purpose. Possum Sauce is kind of a mess. The best thing about Grandma Barrel's costume is her gray pillbox hat, made out of some kind of stringy yarn, with a long possum tail trailing down her neck. She looks *perfect*.

"Grandma Barrel!" I say. "You look—"

"I look like an overgrown rat, dear. But *you* look like a forest warrior, and I am happy to be your sidekick for today."

"Thank you, Grandma Barrel. These costumes are great."

"Yes they are, dear. And now you know how to sew. Do keep in mind this contest isn't a sure thing. Nothing in this life really is. But I've given my best effort, and so have you. Finish your coffee, Margaret. I can't believe your mother lets you drink it. And then let's go to Comic Con."

I take a long gulp of coffee. "I can't believe you decided to dress up, too."

Grandma Barrel flourishes her hand. "When in Rome, Margaret. When in Rome."

I finish my coffee, kiss Mom, Dad, and Aaron goodbye, and wait for our ride share with Grandma Barrel. I'm pretty sure my feet don't touch the ground the entire time.

✖✖✖

The ride share driver looks apologetic once we get within a few blocks of the convention center in Seattle. "I'm sorry, ladies. I'm going to have a hard time getting any closer than this."

I look out the window and see exactly what he means. The streets are filled with people in costumes. There is an entire family dressed up like characters from *Alice in Wonderland*. Even their baby is dressed up like the Cheshire Cat. Four out of six Power Rangers are running down the sidewalk, and I can see the other two waving to them up ahead. There are hundreds of princesses, aliens, ponies, and people wearing Seahawks jerseys. They are all headed in the direction of the convention center.

"No problem," I say to the driver. "Let's go, Grandma Barrel."

Grandma Barrel tips the driver on her phone, and before we both climb out of the car, I hear the driver say, "Coolest grandma *I* ever heard of."

We wade through a sea of mermaids, superheroes, supervillains, and Sasquatches. A man in a green suit with question marks all over it grins at us.

"Eagirl and Possum Sauce!" He nods. "Nice!"

Grandma Barrel smiles a little. "Thank you very much."

When we finally reach the wide glass door of the convention center, I hold my breath. A man with a long beard, burlap robe, and twisted-looking wand opens the door for us, and we step inside. The lobby is bright and loud and colorful, full of costumed and uncostumed fans, and there are signs in front of dozens of doors.

WIZARDVERSE MEET AND GREET

SHARK TWISTER FILM PANEL

SEAHAWKS MEET AND GREET

UNDER THE SEA WITH SHRIMPMAN

AUDITORIUM

BAT KID CAVE

ASK THE DIRECTORS PANEL

EAGIRL'S LAIR

"That's the one." I squeeze Grandma Barrel's arm. "That's where Nora Cho will be."

28

The room marked EAGIRL'S LAIR is the most incredible room I have ever been inside. When we walk through the door, it's like we're walking into an actual forest. Enormous trees fill the room—real trees, like they built the convention center around an actual forest. Pine trees, fir trees, spruce, hemlock, and junipers. Pine cones and dry grass litter the ground. There are flat stone paths to different clearings in the trees that are set up as different Eagirl stations.

One of the clearings is marked COMIC GROVE by twigs arranged into letters on the wall. There are eight bookshelves in Comic Grove, split into two rows like a tiny library in the woods. The shelves are filled with *Exceptional Eagirl* comics.

Down another path in the "forest," there is another clearing marked THE STAGE. The Stage is a large, rustic, wooden platform with a backdrop photo of a mossy riverbank. Eagirl, Possum Sauce, and Grizzly Baird look-alikes pose there under bright lights with a little girl—she looks like she's maybe Aaron's age—and her mom. A photographer in a forest ranger hat takes their picture. Behind the photographer, there is a long line of Eagirl fans waiting to get *their* photos taken. Many of them are dressed in Eagirl costumes. Some of the costumes are exactly alike—they must have bought them from the same store or something.

A third forest path leads to a clearing marked THE CANTEEN, full of Eagirl merchandise. There are T-shirts, umbrellas, water bottles, Ranger Danger forest ranger hats, and Eagirl posters. Dozens of Eagirl fans are lined up like ants, holding fistfuls of money out to workers behind the cash registers.

The last path leads to a far clearing marked PENCIL POINT. I know exactly what I'll find at Pencil Point. I start pulling Grandma Barrel down that path, until we get close enough to see a woman in a green sweater bent over an angled table, drawing. A bright lamp hangs over her. She is surrounded by fans who are watching her draw. Some are actually crying—the tears streaming down their faces sparkle in the light of the overhead lamp.

"Grandma Barrel," I whisper. "That's Nora Cho!"

I want to meet her so badly, but all of a sudden, I am terrified. My heart is beating out of my chest, and I feel a little sick to my stomach. What will I even say to her? *Hi?* Nora Cho writes the best comics in the entire world. She changed my life. She deserves better than *hi*. And anyway, there are at least fifteen Eagirl fans crowded around her, all dressed in identical, expensive-looking Eagirl costumes. I might not get to meet Nora Cho after all. And I am definitely not going to win the costume contest. My heart sinks.

Before I can decide whether I want to squeeze into Pencil Point with the other fans, a man in a forest ranger hat drops his heavy hand on my shoulder. "Eagirl!" he says. "Here to save the day?"

"I, um…What?" My brain is foggy, and my tongue feels like cotton.

The man in the hat thrusts a clipboard at me. "I assume you're going to enter the Best Eagirl Costume contest today?"

"She most certainly is." Grandma Barrel takes the clipboard, removes a ballpoint pen from the metal clip at the top, and writes my name.

"Great, great," says the man. "Because your costume is *awesome*. I love the Possum Sauce element." He nods toward Grandma Barrel. "Head over to the photo wall in about fifteen minutes. That's when Nora Cho is judging. You two look just like Eagirl and Possum Sauce. Good luck."

"We do?" My cheeks get hot.

"We absolutely do," says Grandma Barrel. "Now gather up some courage. You are here to meet your cartoonist."

"*Yeah* you are!" says a very familiar voice.

I look up. LaTanya is headed toward me, winding down a forest path, wearing a blue and green Seahawks jersey.

"LaTanya!" We hug each other tight.

"I knew exactly where to find you. Your hair looks *so* good. If I do say so myself. And your costumes!" She touches the feathers on my shoulder. "Grandma Barrel, you must be the only fan here dressed up as Possum Sauce!" LaTanya nods her head toward the man with the hat and his clipboard. The man is holding his clipboard out toward another Eagirl now, but this Eagirl is wearing a brown tank top and jeans. Fake eagle feathers cover one shoulder, and her hair is in braids like mine—like the real Eagirl—but her costume doesn't look very much like a real Eagirl costume.

"There are a lot of costumes here today," I say. I don't want to say *Costumes that are better than mine* in front of Grandma Barrel, because it would hurt her feelings. And anyway, my costume is beautiful. It just isn't as expensive or detailed as most of those other costumes.

"Let's go meet Nora Cho," says LaTanya.

I take a deep breath. Grandma Barrel squeezes one of my hands, and LaTanya squeezes the other. We walk over to Nora Cho together. There are still ten other people crowded around her, watching her draw the next issue of *Exceptional Eagirl*. Ten finished pages are spread across her desk, and the art is so bright and beautiful that I feel like I can't catch my breath. She draws quickly and gracefully. She takes a sip of her coffee, and I see that it's light. There's milk in it! Nora Cho doesn't drink bitter coffee. She drinks it the same way I do! I watch Eagirl appear, stroke by stroke, on Nora Cho's thick bristol board, until my head feels completely full of helium and I worry I might pass out.

"I really love you," I squeak at Nora Cho's back.

She looks up and turns around. "You do?"

I will myself to turn into a puddle and melt into the floor.

"Uh—I mean, I love Eagirl. I've been reading your comics since I started reading in the first place, and…I mean, I love her. I want to be a forest ranger because of her. That's been my dream since I was like seven."

Nora Cho smiles at me. "I really love hearing that. I always wanted to be a forest ranger, too. I became a comic-book creator instead, but I still—"

Crack.

I feel cold all of a sudden. That sound.

That sound reminds me of the tree at the beginning of the summer. The tree that fell on our old car. The tree that could have *killed* me. I look up at the trees surrounding Nora

Cho's desk. *A ranger would assess the situation.* None of the trees look unhealthy. None of them look like they're going to lose a limb or crack in half.

Crack.

I turn my head toward the sound.

"The lamp!" I yell.

Nora Cho looks at me like she doesn't understand. I point to the hinged lamp over the desk. Nora Cho turns toward it, but she is too late. The hinge lets out again—a second *crack*—and this time the lamp falls on top of Nora Cho's mug of milky coffee with a loud *POP*, smashing the mug and flinging small pieces of light-bulb glass across the desk.

Nora Cho sits, stunned. I hear a few screams from people nearby.

Assess the situation.

Know when to ask for help.

"Nora Cho, your pages!" I yell. She remains still. She is watching the flood of coffee move closer to her unfinished Eagirl page. I snatch it up, careful to avoid the pieces of broken bulb, before it gets ruined. Nora Cho snaps into action too. She scrambles to rescue her other pages.

Assess the situation.

"We need somebody to clean up the glass before anyone gets hurt," I say. "Grandma Barrel, will you—"

"I'm on it!" says Grandma Barrel, and she quickly makes her way out of Pencil Point to find a custodian.

Assess the situation. I look at the crowd of fans stretching their necks to see what's happening.

"I need someone to hold everyone back—no one come any closer. LaTanya, will you find a security guard? They'll need to tape off this whole area, or someone is going to step on a piece of glass."

"You got it." LaTanya disappears. Just thirty seconds later, she returns with a security guard whose name tag says LINDA.

Everybody get back!" Linda yells.

We all step back. Nora Cho stands up, clutching her rescued pages. She turns to look at me and smiles.

"You absolutely saved this next issue of Eagirl. What is your name?"

"Maggie Chowder," I say. My voice sounds croakier than usual.

"Well, Maggie Chowder, thank you. You were amazing." Nora Cho retrieves a pen from her desk before Linda can stop her. "I want you to have this. My way of saying thanks." She scrawls something across one of the bristol boards and hands the page to me.

It's the drawing I watched her work on before the lamp fell! There is a speech bubble next to Eagirl's face. It says,

Thanks for everything, Maggie Chowder. The bottom corner of the page has Nora Cho's unmistakable signature on it.

"Thank you so much," I croak. "I…This is just—"

Nora Cho puts a hand on my shoulder. "Thank *you*. Now I've got a costume contest to MC. Are you entering?"

"Yeah, I—"

"She is," says Grandma Barrel, who has found a custodian. "There's all of that glass and coffee," she says to him, nodding toward Nora Cho's desk. She turns back toward us. "Are you judging the contest?"

"No, no, things like that make me very uncomfortable. Disappointing fans, picking one over another. And anyway, it would be really hard to be impartial after…you know." Nora Cho looks toward the desk. The custodian is sweeping glass into a dustpan.

"But I will see you over at the stage! I'm supposed to meet the judges there in a few minutes."

When Nora Cho walks away, I let out the breath that I was apparently holding.

"Well, that was something," I say to Grandma Barrel and LaTanya.

"*You* were something, Margaret," says Grandma Barrel. "You showed exquisite intuition over there. You assessed the situation and delegated tasks like a true forest ranger. You *should* attend Junior Forest Ranger Camp."

"I want to."

"You *must*," says Grandma Barrel. "Margaret, I've never mentioned this to anyone, but I-I wanted so much to be a forest ranger when I was your age."

A moment ago, I thought Nora Cho handing me an autographed Eagirl page after I saved her new issue from certain doom was the most unlikely thing imaginable.

"*You?*" I remember her name written in *Law Enforcement in Forestry: The Forest Ranger's Handbook.*

Grandma Barrel laughs.

"I suppose it is hard for you to imagine now. It's a dream I gave up a long time ago."

"What happened?" I ask, still shocked. "Why did you give it up?"

"There were many reasons. I didn't try. I chose what I thought was a more sensible path. Don't you dare make the same mistake I did." There are tears in her eyes, and her chin is quivering like she might cry.

I know Grandma Barrel doesn't like hugs, but I throw my arms around her and hug her tight anyway.

"Okay," I say. "I didn't know, Grandma Barrel. I had no idea."

Grandma Barrel squeezes me tight. "We can talk about it later. Let's pull ourselves together, walk over there, and win that contest. You're going to be great, Margaret."

29

I see him as soon as I enter the clearing marked THE STAGE. It's Shrimpman Guy from the comic book store, except he's dressed in a Shrimpman costume, tail and all. The guy who doesn't even *like* Eagirl. So why is he standing on the stage next to Nora Cho and two other women, holding a microphone?

"Okay, Eagirls and boys. Get it? Eagirls and boys? Anyway, if you're signed up to enter the Eagirl costume contest, get up here."

LaTanya holds onto my autographed Eagirl page for me and sits down in the audience. Grandma Barrel links her arm with mine.

"Oh! Are you coming up, too?" I ask.

"Well, yes. Possum Sauce is Eagirl's sidekick, is she not?"

I smile at Grandma Barrel. "She totally is."

Grandma Barrel and I climb the one step to the stage

and line up under the bright lights with nineteen other girls wearing almost identical Eagirl costumes and the one girl wearing a brown tank top, jeans, and feathers.

The Eagirl on my left turns to me. "Was that you who saved the new issue?" she asks. "You're like a real-life superhero."

A real-life Eagirl.

"Thanks," I say. I can tell my cheeks are turning red.

"I mean it," she says. "Those were some good instincts. My name's Mirha."

"Maggie Chowder," I say.

"I'm Nora Cho," says Nora Cho. "Let's get started! Thank you all for coming in your fabulous costumes." She waves her hand toward the judges. "These are the judges who will choose our winner."

"The only reason I'm here is because my Shrimpman event ended early due to low attendance," says Shrimpman Guy, leaning over Nora Cho's microphone, "and I owe the convention folks another hour of work to cover my free badge."

This guy is the *worst.*

Nora Cho pulls the microphone close to her mouth and paces the stage so Shrimpman Guy can't borrow it again. "As you know, the winner of the Eagirl costume contest will be awarded a full scholarship to Junior Forest Ranger Camp."

All of the Eagirls on the stage squeal in excitement.

"Okay, judges. Let's do it," says Nora Cho.

The judges step off the stage and sit down behind a long folding table in front of the audience.

Nora Cho steps down, too, and sits in a front-row seat with a reserved sign on it.

The judges study us for a minute. I suddenly feel uncomfortable, like I have something on my face. I have no idea what my hands should be doing. I try to slide them into my pockets, but remember too late that I don't have pockets.

I look at Grandma Barrel. She is looking at me. And suddenly, a laugh bursts out of me. I cover my mouth with my hand, but it's too late. Now Grandma Barrel is turning pink and shaking. She's laughing too. I pinch myself to stop giggling, but I can't stop. Until I look at the judges. They're all looking at me.

After what seems like forever, Nora Cho gets back on the stage. An assistant in a Ranger Danger hat hands her a piece of paper. My throat feels tight. I bet that piece of paper is the scholarship to Junior Forest Ranger Camp. "Are the judges ready?"

"We're ready," says Shrimpman Guy.

"Excellent. I'll let you do the honors." Nora Cho hands him the microphone.

"Well," says Shrimpman Guy, "we had a clear winner."

He looks at all twenty-one of us, plus Grandma Barrel. "Look...You all look the same. I mean, there is a serious lack of creativity here. Most of you bought the same costume." He points at the girl in the tank top and jeans. "Well, not you. You probably *should* have bought the same costume. Your outfit barely *counts* as a costume. It's just clothes. *This* is a costume." He wiggles his Shrimpman tail.

The girl in the tank top and jeans rolls her eyes and steps down off the stage.

"But *you*..." Shrimpman Guy is pointing at me. At *me!* "You took your presentation to another level. Your costume is original. It doesn't look like everybody else's. It looks like you put work into it. And you have a sidekick!" He gestures toward Grandma Barrel. "What's Eagirl without Possum Sauce?"

I look at Grandma Barrel. Her eyes are twinkling.

Nora Cho approaches the judges' table and whispers back and forth with the judges for a few seconds. Then she straightens, steps up to the stage, and raises the microphone.

"First of all, let's give all our contestants a big hand!"

The contestants and audience all clap politely while Nora Cho slowly walks the stage in front of us.

"This was a great contest and you were all wonderful, but we only have one scholarship to award, and that goes to..."

She stops in front of me and hands me the piece of paper.

"Congratulations, Maggie Chowder, you're going to Junior Forest Ranger Camp."

Everyone in the audience stands up, claps, and cheers. I can hear LaTanya clapping and cheering loudest of all. Grandma Barrel is beaming at me. She looks proud and excited. There are goose bumps all over my arms.

Mirha squeals. "Congratulations, Maggie!" She reaches out and squeezes my hand.

"Thanks, Mirha! I'm sorry that, uh…"

"Oh, don't even worry about it," says Mirha. "I literally go to Junior Forest Ranger Camp every summer, scholarship or no scholarship. I'll see you there in a few weeks!"

Wow. Mirha must be really lucky.

But right now, I feel really lucky, too.

"See you there," I say.

✕✕✕

My hands shake all the way to the taco place inside the convention center. I can tell they're shaking, because the scholarship and autographed Eagirl page I'm carrying are shaking.

Grandma Barrel, LaTanya, and I had no idea how hungry we were until the contest was over.

The restaurant is packed, and we are at least twentieth in line to order.

"Do they have a sandwich?" asks Grandma Barrel, who is wincing at the giant light-up menu behind the counter.

"No," I say. "They have tacos. Can you believe Nora Cho *gave* this to me?"

"Can you believe you're going to Junior Forest Ranger Camp?" squeals LaTanya. "This is a *really* big deal!"

"Do they have a soup?"

"Grandma Barrel, everything they have is right there on the menu. They don't have soup. They have tacos." I look at LaTanya. "And I know! It's a really, really big deal. I can't even believe it. This day has been *wild*."

"Do they have a submarine sandwich?"

"What am I gonna do without you when you're at camp for two weeks?" LaTanya asks softly. "Hang out in my empty house and watch TV with Glitter?"

I squeeze LaTanya's hand. "You could always come with me to Junior Forest Ranger Camp, you know," I say. "We could pick up forest litter together. Identify types of animal poop. Listen to bird calls in the rain. Scrape moss off of cabin steps."

LaTanya's face breaks into a smile. "Okay, you got a point. I'm going to hang out in my empty house and watch TV with Glitter. And not get rained on or sniff bear poop."

"Do they have a chicken breast?" asks Grandma Barrel.

30

Grandma Barrel and I are quiet in the back seat of our ride share on the way home. It starts raining lightly, and the trees we pass seem a brighter green than they did this morning. I read my scholarship letter over and over until I start to feel carsick. Then I look at my Eagirl drawing from Nora Cho. I can't believe it's real. I can't believe *any* of it is real. I can't believe I'm going to the camp I have dreamed of going to for so long.

Maybe Dad really wasn't wrong. Maybe this *is* the summer of our dreams coming true.

The car pulls up in front of our apartment building, and we both climb out. I look up at the building that seemed beige and gray and not at all like home for most of this summer. But it *is* home. The people in there—Mom, Dad, and Aaron—are the people I'm most excited to tell about what happened today. About my scholarship.

Home used to be our big house with its own yard. Now home is an apartment where I have to climb a bunch of steps to get to the front door. It's got a dumpster just below my bedroom window, so it smells like garbage, especially on hot days. It's got a balcony overlooking a massive tangle of invasive blackberry vines. It's got a not-so-bad-after-all cranky Grandma Barrel sleeping on the couch. It's got green crocodile face paint still in some of the grout in the bathroom.

When we get to the top of the steps, the front door flings open and Aaron is standing there.

"Maggie is Eagirl today," he says. "I am Aaron. Grandma Barrel is…" He looks at Grandma Barrel behind me. He sticks his tongue out one side of his mouth like he does when he's thinking. "Grandma Barrel is rat."

"'Grandma Barrel is rat,'" says Grandma Barrel. "Why not. What do you say we watch *Diagnosis Murder* after I change out of my rat clothes, Aaron?"

"I like *Diagnosis Murder*," says Aaron.

xxx

LaTanya's parents drop her off at my apartment before dinner.

"Listen," she says, hanging her denim jacket in the coat closet. "If you're going to leave me for two weeks, I'm going to be here a *lot* before then."

"Good!" I say. "I like when you're here. But bring Glitter next time." My apartment doesn't allow dogs to *live* here, but the website doesn't say anything about dogs not being allowed to visit.

At the dinner table, Mom and Dad gush over my scholarship.

"This is incredible, Mags," says Dad. "You're going to have a blast. Do you think you can get Smokey Bear's autograph for me?"

"I'll see what I can do."

"Speaking of autographs, Mr. Chowder, do you think you could get the *Lyle* cast to sign my copy of *Lyle, Lyle, Crocodile?*" asks LaTanya. "I'll bring it next time I come over."

Dad's face lights up. He puts his fork down. "I'll do you one better, LaTanya. We're reading for season two pretty soon. Why don't you tag along with me to an audition? You can hang out with the cast, and even try out if you want."

LaTanya's mouth drops open. "*Me?* Is there an available kid's role? Do you think I have a chance at it? Thank you, Mr. Chowder!"

Maybe it *is* kind of cool that my dad plays a crocodile on the internet. My chest fills up with the same proud feeling I had on the night of the premiere.

"Is that pavlova I saw in the refrigerator?" asks Grandma Barrel.

"It is!" Mom beams. "I had some time this afternoon, and I wanted to try out some new desserts for the bakery."

"Lucky us!" says Dad.

Grandma Barrel smiles at Mom. "I'm very proud of you, Heidi."

"I know." Mom smiles back at Grandma Barrel, then turns to me. "We're going to have to make your packing list pretty soon, Maggie. I'm so excited for you." She sighs. "But I keep thinking about that lamp! I mean, what is it with you and falling *stuff*?"

"Margaret reacted like a true forest ranger today. She followed her instincts. And instincts are a forest ranger's most important asset."

"Thanks for everything, Grandma Barrel." I bet Grandma Barrel would have made a really great forest ranger.

"You know, I won't be here for much longer. I fly back to Arizona in just over a week. But I expect you to write to me about your time at Junior Forest Ranger Camp. I will live vicariously through you."

"I'll write, I promise."

Grandma Barrel reaches over and squeezes my hand.

"Are you going to miss me when I go to camp, Aaron? What will you do without me for two weeks?" I ask.

Aaron finishes chewing the food in his mouth. "I am going to play with Eva." He stabs a noodle with his fork.

"I am going to go to OT and speech. I am going to watch *Diagnosis Murder*. I am going to make lists."

"Oh. You've got your own plans, then."

Aaron looks at me thoughtfully. "I have my own plans."

"Speaking of Eva and *Diagnosis Murder*," says Mom, "Ma, Eva's mother is dropping Eva off tomorrow evening, and she's asked me *not* to let her watch *Diagnosis Murder* anymore. It's been giving her nightmares."

Grandma Barrel sighs. "Fine." She takes a sip of water. "Aaron doesn't have nightmares, do you, Aaron." She doesn't say it like she's really asking.

"Is Eva's mom doing more errands?" I ask.

"It sounds like...Actually, she is going on a date." Mom blushes a little.

"With Mr. Primms himself! Dag told me he's been seeing Eva's mom," says Dad.

LaTanya and I share a look.

"Dahhhling," LaTanya whispers. "You *must* be an actress."

"*The summer of our dreams coming true*." I stick a forkful of pasta into my mouth. "I guess it's the summer of *everybody's* dreams coming true."

"Don't talk with your mouth full, dear," says Grandma Barrel.

Dad stands up to clear off the table. He takes my plate

and Aaron's, and places them in the sink with a quiet rattle.

"I have my own plans," says Aaron.

xxx

LaTanya's dad picks her up after dinner, and Mom gives Aaron his bath. Dad has to work on lines for the next *Lyle* episode, so I join Grandma Barrel on the balcony. She is looking out over the blackberry vines with a mug of tea. I sit down in the chair next to her, and we don't say anything for a few minutes. It is raining, but not hard. Just enough to rustle the blackberry leaves and make everything sparkle. In this moment, sitting with Grandma Barrel on our balcony, I can't imagine wanting to be anywhere else. Not in our old house with the big yard. Not in LaTanya's new house with the bushes shaped like tigers and dolphins. I feel okay being right here.

ACKNOWLEDGMENTS

I want to thank my husband, Zach, who read countless drafts of this book, worked some editing magic, and believed in Maggie Chowder as much as I did. When I was up late editing, he swooped in with tea and encouragement, and those are the exact things I need in order to finish a book.

Thank you to my agent, Samantha Wekstein, for being truly awesome, answering all of my excessive questions, and rooting for Maggie. I got really lucky, here. Thank you to Meg Thompson and Thompson Literary Agency, and thank you to Cindy Uh for loving Maggie in the first place.

Thank you to Christina Pulles for making Maggie Chowder a part of the Albert Whitman & Company family, and for being the most phenomenal editor. Thank you to Albert Whitman & Company! This still feels like a dream. I've loved your books my whole life, and I feel incredibly lucky that Maggie Chowder gets to be among them.

Thank you to Luna Valentine, who is just wickedly talented. I am so glad that Maggie (and Eagirl, Possum Sauce, Grizz, Ranger Danger, etc.) are yours to draw!

Thank you to Sheila O'Connor, my grad school advisor who continues to advise me, nearly a decade after graduation. She once sent me a message that said, "The writers who make it are the writers who stay in it," and I think of that all the time.

Writing books and raising three young kids at the same time is a really hard thing to do. Awesome, but hard. I wouldn't be able to do it without Evangeline OpongParry, who hangs out with my kids so I can get a few uninterrupted hours of writing done a week. I wouldn't be able to do it without my mom, Lisa Beauregard, who flies out for a few weeks at a time when I have a deadline so I can get the writing done.

Thank you to Tara Jesson and Grace Kershaw at Sound Children's Therapy who answered all of my questions and read the OT chapter for accuracy. Thanks, also, for being such cool people in Simon's life.

Thank you to Becky Sosby, for lending me your Pacific Northwest trail and travel guides, for being a major source for all of my PNW information, and for encouraging me and Maggie Chowder the whole way.

Thank you to my critique group, for reading so many drafts of so many of these chapters and providing fantastic feedback. Barrett, Ann Strawn, Laura Barfield, and Lenae Nofziger, I appreciate you so much.

And thank you to Lindsey Stirling, whose music I listened to constantly and exclusively while I wrote this book.